THE
ANTI-INJUSTICE
SQUAD
THE CACOMISTLE TEAM

KENT JOHNSON OLSEN

ARCHWAY
PUBLISHING

Archway Publishing books may be ordered through booksellers or by contacting:

Archway Publishing
1663 Liberty Drive
Bloomington, IN 47403
www.archwaypublishing.com
1 (888) 242-5904

Because of the dynamic nature of the Internet, any web addresses or
links contained in this book may have changed since publication and
may no longer be valid. The views expressed in this work are solely those
of the author and do not necessarily reflect the views of the publisher,
and the publisher hereby disclaims any responsibility for them.

Any people depicted in stock imagery provided by Thinkstock are models,
and such images are being used for illustrative purposes only.
Certain stock imagery © Thinkstock.

ISBN: 978-1-4808-5818-3 (sc)
ISBN: 978-1-4808-5817-6 (e)

Library of Congress Control Number: 2018901246

Print information available on the last page.

Archway Publishing rev. date: 1/31/2018

Contents

Every person born on this earth
has the right to walk through life
unmolested, unafraid.
—Sensei J. R. Jensen, 1981

Be SAFE. Practice martial arts in a dojo (studio) with a TRAINED and CERTIFIED sensei or martial arts instructor.

Acknowledgments: To Sensei J. R. Jensen, teacher and friend, who brought balance to my life.

To Kathy Kinnard, who reads and gives great comments on content, grammar, and spelling.

Dedicated to: John, Rebecca, Jessica, Riley, Amanda, Ethan, and Aiden. Good friends. Characters:

Riley Whirl, 18 – she needs money and training
Terry Whirl, 19 – willing to lend a hand
Donna, 44 – J Bar J cook, housekeeper, wrangler
Lila Brown, 20 – roommate to Riley, proficient martial artist
Zeke, 22 – Aztec, guide
Nathan Baker, 21 – team member, Lila's boyfriend
John Johnson, 33 – owner of J Bar J Dude Ranch
Roy, 22 – speed is his attitude
Chet, 20 – has three black belts
Betty, 18 – has been training since age eight
Clara, 10 – forced to work by slavers
Danni, 11 – field worker only a few days
Jake Logan, 38 – his business is greenbacks
Tommy, 24 – Logan's right-hand man
Allen, 24 – twin to Tommy
Chip, 18 – ruffian
Eddie, 19 – ruffian
Jim, 18 – ruffian
Katie, MD – a helper for John's team
Lt Jim Mack – police assigned to special projects
Detective Tiffany Smith – police work is her passion.

CHAPTER 1

J Bar J Ranch

One person makes a difference.
A team makes many variances.
—Sensei J. R. Jensen

Riley Whirl stepped off the interstate bus in Dudleyville, near Payson. Barely eighteen years old, her tall, slender figure filled worn jeans, a white blouse, and threadbare sneakers. Brown hair flowed onto her shoulders and covered the right side of her face. Her visible green eye scanned the area.

In her hand, Riley held a telegram that read:

Welcome to J Bar J Health Ranch. Stop.
Sorry your dad lost his job. Stop.
You start work when you arrive. Stop.
Tell no one I am your uncle. Stop.
John Johnson.

Entering the convenience store, Riley approached the cashier. "Can you tell me where the J Bar J is?" she asked.

The cashier pointed out the door. "It's three miles, honey."

Riley left the store and hiked in the direction of the ranch, her suitcase in hand and her backpack firmly in place on her back.

The cashier watched the girl leave. Then, picking up the

telephone, she dialed a local number and spoke into the phone. "Another girl walking to the J Bar J." She hung up.

As Riley walked along, she saw a red barn with J Bar J on its roof in the distance. Teams of young men and women ran along the fence line. A rumbling reached her ears, and she turned to see a green pickup speeding up the road toward her. Shrugging, she turned around to see no one running along the fence line. "Now what happened to those runners?" she asked aloud.

Finally, she reached the main gate to the J Bar J. A sign announced it as a health and fitness ranch. Reaching to open the gate, she stood face-to-face with a giant mastiff. Riley backed up, blinking. The dog just watched her. "Now what do I do?" she asked herself.

The 1951 green Studebaker pickup pulled up behind her and stopped. "Well, another chick for the dude ranch," said a voice. "What's yer tag, chick?"

Riley turned around and faced three scruffily dressed young men. Her hair fell away from the right side of her face, revealing burned, scarred, ugly skin.

"Hey, look at the ugly chick," said the tallest young man, who had noticeably large ears. He jumped off the back of the truck and grabbed Riley's suitcase. He opened it and dumped the few clothing items on the mowed grass.

Riley quickly covered her scarred face with her hair.

Big Ears stepped behind Riley. He was easily twice her size. He wrapped his arms around her and her backpack in a bear hug. Riley shifted her body to her right, hit Big Ears in the groin with her left hand, and, moving her left foot behind his right foot, stood up.

Big Ears flew onto his back and landed, gasping for breath. He tried to get up and failed, falling back onto the ground. Rolling over, he finally managed to stand.

A shrill whistle sounded.

Immediately, the mastiff jumped the fence and growled at Big Ears, who moved backward away from the dog so fast he tripped over the suitcase, lost his balance, and fell again on the cut grass by the fence.

From the trees, four athletic young men and two slim young women dropped to the ground between Big Ears and Riley and her suitcase.

Riley quickly stuffed her things back in the suitcase, closed it, and stood, watching the ruffians. She kept her hair over her face while glancing back at the six young men and women standing behind her. They all wore J Bar J sweatshirts.

"Where did you come from?" Riley asked.

"Tell you later," said a blonde girl in pigtails.

The mastiff grabbed the suitcase handle in its mouth. Riley let the dog have the suitcase. The dog walked over and patiently waited by the gate.

An athletic Aztec dropped with ease out of the tree and stood between Riley and the ruffians.

"Open the gate and step in," instructed then Aztec, gently pushing Riley toward the gate. Riley hurried to open the gate. The mastiff slipped through the gate and trotted toward the ranch house. "Close the gate behind you," he instructed.

"We'll get you, Aztec," yelled Big Ears, moving to stand by his friends.

Riley swiftly entered the gate, closed it, and turned to watch.

The Aztec turned and did a running dive over the barbed-wire fence, rolled into a standing position, and broke into a mile-eating trot toward the main house on the property.

"Now, Chip," called a voice behind Riley, "behave."

Riley turned to see a tall, slender woman in western wear. "Who are you?" she asked.

"I'm Donna, cook, housekeeper, and when I get John in a good mood, a wrangler," she said.

Two German shepherds ran up to the fence and growled at the young men.

The three ruffians jumped into their truck and sped away.

"Local troublemakers, Eddie, Jim, and Chip," said Donna. "Chip is the one with the large ears."

"I'm Riley Whirl. I got Mr. Johnson's telegram."

"Welcome, young lady. We've been expecting you. Come with me." Donna turned and followed the mastiff.

"Everyone, thanks for rescuing me." Riley laughed, following Donna.

The group entered the gate and continued their jog around the fence line as if nothing had happened. The mastiff dropped the suitcase at the front door and trotted off. Riley picked up her suitcase when she reached the door, wiping the dog slobber off on her pant leg.

As they entered the ranch house, another girl approached. "Riley, this is Lila Brown. You will be working with her on all assignments. Now, I'm off to finish cooking dinner. Fifteen minutes!" Donna waved.

"Hi," said Lila. Her brown skin was set off by the J Bar J Ranch outfit, consisting of a western blouse and skirt, waist purse, western boots, scarf, and sombrero. Her blonde hair was in a ponytail. Blue eyes completed a perfect picture.

"Were you at the fence just now?" asked Riley.

"Yes, I was."

"Didn't you have pigtails?"

"Yes."

"Nice clothes."

"You'll wear them a lot, and they're really comfortable. Now come, I'll show you to our room."

"Roommates?" asked Riley.

"What else?" Lila laughed.

The two girls strode through the cafeteria into an area marked "staff only."

"We are staff only. Follow the footsteps on the floor to our room for a quick shower. Dress in your uniform with your new western boots, and it's time to eat," Lila said.

"Great. I'm famished."

Riley walked the footsteps down a hall. She found a room labeled "Lila and Riley." After a quick shower, Riley put on the clothes set out on a bed. Socks and cowboy boots completed the outfit. Pulling on her boots, Riley wondered, *Now, how did they get my boot size right?*

***

Donna, Lila, and Riley sat at the kitchen table; two young men entered, dressed in J Bar J western shirts, blue jeans, and western boots.

Donna introduced them. "Zeke you have already seen. The tall one is Turtle."

"Hi," said Turtle. "My name is really Nathan Baker."

"We call him that because he is so slow." Lila giggled.

"Me? Slow?" said Nathan.

Lila whispered in Riley's ear, "He's my boyfriend. I had to light a firecracker to get him to notice me."

"Oh," whispered Riley. "What happened to the other workers?"

"They left on assignment," Lila whispered back.

Almost immediately, a slender, medium-height man entered the kitchen. His western clothing looked crisp and sharp. A finely trimmed moustache set off his face. "Good afternoon, staff," said John Johnson, owner of J Bar J.

"Good afternoon, Mr. Johnson," echoed the staff.

"Mr. Johnson, this is Riley Whirl, our newest staff member," said Donna.

"Welcome, Riley. When dinner is finished, we will follow our regular Wednesday schedule," said John with a wink at Riley.

Donna stood and brought in food from the kitchen on a wheeled cart. She placed platters filled with steaks, potatoes and gravy, new peas, tossed green salad, and dietary salad dressing before each person.

John bowed his head. "Lord, for that which we are about to receive, may we truly be thankful. Amen."

"Amen," chorused the staff.

Riley just watched and listened.

The group dug into the repast. Forks busily moved from plate to mouth.

"Please pass the salt," said Riley.

"Everyone duck," cautioned John.

Instantly, the salt shaker flew through the air and landed in Riley's glass of water. The resulting fountain splashed all over her food, her blouse, and the tablecloth.

"Oops, sorry," said Nathan, running around the table to clean up his mess.

Donna handed Riley her napkin. "Nathan likes to play practical jokes," said Donna, frowning.

Riley looked stunned. Then she began to laugh. "I've never received salt sent air mail before."

Laughter filled the table.

Donna got another plate, filled it, and passed it to Riley.

Nathan grimaced and shrugged. "Sorry."

"The blouse will dry," Lila whispered to Riley.

"Why do we eat so many calories?" asked Riley.

"At J Bar J, you burn a lot of calories," replied Lila.

When dinner was over, Donna led Riley to the office, where she gave her several sheets of paper, a pen, and a clipboard.

"Medical history?" queried Riley.

"We're off to see the doctor," said Donna.

A few minutes later, Donna and Riley drove off in a J Bar J Blazer.

***

Hours later, Riley shook her head as she entered the ranch house. "That was a thorough medical exam."

Lila met Riley at the door and guided her to their room, where they rested for exactly thirty minutes. Then, after putting on sweat suits, they walked to the first barn, where the other staff assembled.

John appeared and handed Riley a large loose-leaf binder. "Just watch and read. When your medical exam results are returned, you will be able to join us," he said. "The staff knows about the house fire and your physical scars. You will find them excellent companions."

The staff, with sheriff's deputies, began a series of physical exercises, including sit-ups, push-ups, pull-ups, squat thrusts, balancing on each leg, and aerobic dance steps. The workout lasted a full hour, including the warm-up and cool down periods.

"Wow," said Riley, "do we do this often?" She put on a ribbon to keep her hair out of her eyes. The scars on her face came into full view.

"Only six days a week," Lila said with a smile, wiping her forehead.

"Do we always have sheriff's deputies at our workouts?"

"We do. John trained the sheriff and most of his deputies."

Donna directed the girls to the weight room.

"Oh my, look at all the equipment," said Riley.

Lila looked at Donna and smiled.

"We will test your ability to use the 'equipment,' as you call it," said Donna.

"And only six days a week," said Lila, rolling her eyes.

"Night and morning." Donna giggled. "You will be doing light workouts until JJ says you can get serious. In other words, when the doctor's report says you are alive and breathing, you begin to train in earnest."

Riley took a deep breath. "I can hardly wait to get started."

Back in their room, Lila showered. Lila showed Riley how to set out clothing for the next day. She placed her dirty clothing in a basket outside the room. "We do this every night."

It was ten o'clock when lights went out. The two girls were immediately asleep.

***

The alarm rang at 7:00 a.m. sharp. Riley turned off the noise and got up. Lila was nowhere to be seen, and her bed was made.

Riley made her bed and put on the sweat clothes laid out on her dresser.

Lila knocked and poked her head into the room.

"The doctor called. You are alive and breathing, so let's stretch and go for our morning run," she said.

Riley followed her outside. The stretching exercises took nearly one hour. Lila finished her reverse push-ups and sat on the ground. She put her running-shoe soles together, leaned forward, and stood up, ankles still touching the ground.

"How can you do that?" Riley asked.

"It's called a butterfly stand." Lila stepped out of her leaning stance and stood up.

Patiently, Lila went through the steps. Riley tried but failed miserably several times.

"Never mind. With practice, you'll be able to do it too." Lila began a slow jog; Riley quickly caught up.

"Your exercises work the muscles better than any program I've seen," said Riley.

"What do you say we run around the fence line?" asked Lila.

"You're on," Riley agreed.

The two kept the same slow jog. Shortly, the two German shepherds joined them, followed by the mastiff.

After they had gone halfway around, Lila stopped. "Put your hands out, palms up. Let the dogs sniff you."

Riley obeyed. The dogs came over and sniffed her hands.

"Now the dogs won't attack you, but they will defend you if anyone tries to hurt you. They're called Corky and Jinx," puffed Lila. "The mastiff is called Piglet."

Riley's musical laughter filled the air. "I haven't laughed so hard since before my dad lost his job and we lost our house."

***

Donna put breakfast on the table, just as Lila and Riley finished their run and entered the kitchen. "Good timing," she said.

The cellular phone rang. Donna answered, and Lila went to the computer.

Donna spoke. "Water retrieved. Arrived Campsite II. Number two has a small cut on left calf."

Lila typed into the computer.

The threesome sat down to bacon, sausage, eggs, toast and strawberry jam, milk, orange juice, plus pancakes and hash browns.

"I'll bet our guests would like to be eating here rather than in the desert," said Lila.

"What do they eat in the desert?" inquired Riley.

"Whatever they can catch, dig up, or scrounge," said Donna with a wicked smile. "It's nice not to have to cook for an extra twenty guests."

CHAPTER 2

Guests

Martial arts training hurts.
Accept the pain. Now you are prepared.
—Sensei J.R. Jensen

At 8:30 a.m., the wilderness party straggled into the barn, where the staff's daily exercises were about to begin.

Immediately, all staff members rushed to stand in a line. Lila pulled Riley into line beside her.

"Welcome, weary guests. We are here to serve you. Take a shower, change into clean clothes, and report for breakfast," said John Johnson. "Holiday schedule is in effect now that our guests are here."

Riley followed Lila into the dining room.

Donna had outdone herself. There was every kind of breakfast food imaginable for the guests: bacon, sausage, eggs sunny side up, eggs sunny side down, scrambled eggs, waffles, pancakes, biscuits, white gravy, bananas, apples, green grapes, red grapes, apple juice, orange juice, pomegranate juice, two-percent milk, whole milk, buttermilk, and soymilk.

"Why the pomegranate juice?" asked Riley.

"It's for the men," said Lila.

Riley looked confused.

"It's for the men to keep fit and trim."

Riley still had a puzzled look on her face.

Lila just laughed.

The guests entered the dining room and filled their plates buffet style. They sat, ate, and talked about their experiences during the week.

"Does anyone need more food?" asked Donna after the guests pushed their plates back and slid their chairs away from the table.

A chorus of satisfied no's filled the air.

"Good. Now I can get ready for lunch." She pushed the kitchen door open and disappeared.

John Johnson stood at his place at the head of the table. "We have had a good week, topped off by a good outing. Do I hear any questions or comments?"

Riley listened with interest.

"Where do you get such good woodsmen and women?" asked a tall guest with white hair.

"I train them myself," said John with a smile. "But I also use the talents of our Aztec brothers."

Lila stood, whistled, and clapped her hands. "Excellent job, wilderness scouts," she said.

The guests enthusiastically clapped with her.

John held up his hands. "This breakfast signals the end of your time with us. We appreciate you and welcome you back anytime."

The guests clapped again, pushed their chairs further back, stood up, and moved to the living room to collect their luggage.

"The vans will depart for the train, bus, and airport in thirty minutes," said John.

***

The vans pulled out of the ranch and turned toward town thirty minutes later. The staff went straight to the living room and selected their favorite easy chair.

John Johnson entered the room. "Let's start our debriefing with a well-done to all who assisted this group of guests."

All staff clapped and whistled.

A knock sounded at the door.

"Come in," said John.

A sloppily dressed young man with shaggy hair, baggy pants, dirty sweatshirt, and very dirty galoshes entered the room.

"Roy, give us a demonstration," said John.

Roy took off his shaggy wig, baggy pants, dirty sweatshirt, and galoshes. He stood up with clean-cut, well-styled hair, short-sleeved shirt, pressed pants, and clean running shoes. He bowed and sat down.

"You will use disguises in the course of your training and assignments," said John.

Donna appeared with a tray full of vegetable drinks all around. "Get them while they're cold," she said.

When everyone had a cold drink in their hand, John pointed to Lila, who turned out the lights.

Using a remote control, John turned on the television. The staff members watched themselves greet guests; assist with teaching guests to saddle a horse; eat meals with the guests at the ranch and in the wild; catch, prepare, cook, and devour wild birds and animals; return to the ranch; eat the final breakfast; and leave in the vans.

"Any suggestions or ideas on how to make their next stay more pleasant?" asked John. He waited for his staff to begin the conversation.

"They liked the food here at the ranch," Donna said.

"They learned to survive in a desert environment and what it takes to find water," Zeke said.

"How can you be sure to have birds and animals available for the guests in the wild?" Riley asked.

"We raise our own animals and birds here at the ranch," said John.

"How?" asked Riley.

"We have three staff members who work with horses and burros. They also raise various game birds and smaller animals for our guests," said John.

"So, you stack or place animals to ensure our guests have food?"

"We do."

Riley stroked her chin.

"I found a man afraid of a rattlesnake. On the third day, he was willing to eat one. He overcame a real fear," Chet said.

"Do you provide rattlesnakes?" asked Riley.

The entire group chuckled.

"No. We rely on nature to provide a few critters."

"The wilderness guests commented how they loved the wild. Many of them had been here before and said they learn new things each time they take the trip," Lila said.

John rose. "Let me introduce Riley, our newest staff member. She will be training with our specialist team."

"John, do we have any reason to trust her with our special assignments?" asked Chet.

"We do. I taught her as a teenager, nearly three years. She completed levels nine, eight, and seven. Any other comments?"

"How long will she need to be in training before we can use her in an operation?" asked Betty.

John took a deep breath and sighed. "We will know in the next two days. If she can handle the training, she will go with us on assignments, on a trial basis at first."

John's glance swept over his staff. "We will be wearing disguises in three days. Lila will dress Riley."

***

In the roommates' room, Riley sat on the bed talking with Lila.

"What did John mean about a disguise?"

Lila looked Riley in the eyes. "John gave you a great compliment. You are the first girl he has taken in as a team member without having at least four months' training here at the ranch. And I'll be putting you in your disguise."

"I trained with him for nearly three years, but that was over six months ago," said Riley.

"We need trained people to help us." Lila pulled out a scrapbook and pointed to a newspaper article. The headline read: "Mysterious group foils gas station robbers."

Lila turned another page.

The headline read: "Ruffians wrapped up for the police by unknown vigilantes."

"You are saying John has us stop crime in this area?" asked Riley.

"Yes, and it goes further than that. John wants us to be shadow crime fighters. The ruffians suspect the police have a snitch in their organization who sends messages to thwart their attempts to steal, but they aren't sure who it is. We have a mole in the ruffian organization who informs us when a robbery is about to happen. John gives the police and us instructions on how to stop the crime and stay alive."

Riley pondered and nodded. "You are a clandestine operation, right?"

"Right. Let's go inventory our equipment," said Lila.

"Inventory?"

"John insists we keep all our supplies checked and ready for action. It's good advice."

Riley followed Lila down to the lower barn and into the equipment room.

Opening a large locker, Lila pulled out and placed everything on a table.

"Notice there is two of everything. Car travel, air travel, desert, mountain, tropic, train, and woodland packs," she said.

"And I thought I had received most of John's training," said Riley, shaking her head.

"We use the mountain packs when we search for a missing child. John told me to teach you about the air-travel and train-travel packs."

"Air and train? Does that mean we are going flying and traveling on a train?"

"You know John's motto, don't you?"

"Sure, *be ready.*"

Lila pulled out two packs. "These are the air-travel and train packs." She pulled a jacket out of the pack and helped Riley put it on.

"It's a lot heavier than it looks," said Riley.

"John insists we wear this jacket when on any aircraft. And we must wear the boots when we wear any jacket." Lila pulled out a pair of boots. She turned the right boot over and pulled off the heel. In the heel was a square wrapped in foil. Lila unwrapped the foil to reveal fishing line, hooks, two fishing lures, and a miniature knife. From a second foil, Lila pulled out a full-body emergency blanket.

"Just in case we find ourselves in a desperate situation."

Lila then pulled off the left boot heel and removed three quarters and two folded twenty-dollar bills. "One of the quarters is a homing device provided by the Homeland Security people. Notice I can pull out the shank that gives strength to the sole of each boot. They are serrated on one side and sharpened on the other."

"Just what kind of situation are we preparing for?" asked Riley.

"You can feed yourself, make animal traps, fish, keep warm, and activate the homing device to be found."

"When do we practice using the equipment?"

"In two weeks, John will run us through all the equipment, including the parachute jacket you said was heavy." Lila smirked.

"The jacket serves as a real parachute?"

"Have you flown an airplane before?"

"No."

"You will, and you'll be able to pack a parachute before training is done. JJ's training is very thorough."

"I believe it," said Riley.

Lila put on the jacket and zipped it up. She grabbed hold of the epaulets on the shoulder pads and pulled. The room filled with a parachute, pushing the girls against the locker.

"Wow!" Riley said with a laugh.

"Put on your jacket." Lila folded her parachute on the table and slipped it back into the jacket.

Riley put on her parachute jacket and zipped it up.

"Now reach up and grab the epaulets. Pull gently until you can get your thumb in the end holes and get a good grip."

Riley followed the instructions.

"Good. Now pull hard."

Riley pulled. Nothing happened.

"Pull with all your strength."

Riley pulled. The parachute opened and filled the room again.

"That's great. Now put the parachute on the table," said Lila. "You will use it when you jump, fall, or get pushed out of an airplane."

"Really? You said *when*. Does that mean we will use the parachute in the future?"

"Oh, yes. Let's use the tabletop to pack this chute and put it back in your jacket," said Lila. "Come, I'll teach you."

CHAPTER 3

Mountain Rescue

Always protect women and children,
for they are our present and future.
—Sensei J. R. Jensen

Donna walked into the living room with a cell phone. "It's the sheriff. He says it's urgent."

John took the phone. "Hello, Sheriff." He listened a few seconds and then hung up the phone. All eyes were on his face.

"A six-year-old girl is lost in Squaw Peak Park. Plan for a twenty-four-hour search. Lila and Riley will use Corky. Roy and Chet will use Jinx. Betty will handle communications with the vans. Move," said John Johnson.

The room cleared at once.

Lila guided Riley to the exercise barn. They went into the women's locker room, where Lila unlocked a gray cabinet marked "Rescue."

"Change into the search outfits," she said.

The two young women put on camouflage pants and shirts. Two full backpacks sat on top of each other in the cabinet.

"Each pack contains survival supplies for three days for two people, plus a first-aid kit and emergency blankets," said Lila, putting on her pack and changing into boots she pulled from the cabinet.

Riley put on her outfit, including the boots.

"Your training includes wearing a light jacket with a pack during a local operation, which gives confidence and emergency supplies if the worst happens," said Lila.

Riley reached into the locker, pulled out a jacket and pack at random, and put them on.

Forty-five minutes later, two J Bar J vans arrived at the Squaw Peak Park visitor's center.

Lila jumped out of the van, ran over, and gave the sheriff a hug. "Hi, Daddy."

"Lila, we really need to find this child."

"We'll do our best."

Riley blinked. "The sheriff is your dad?"

"I'm the youngest of ten children," said Lila.

Sheriff Able Brown approached and shook John's hand as he stepped out of the van. The sheriff was a corpulent man in his fifties; white hair peeked out from under his cap.

"Here is the fanny pack little Tina Rodriguez was wearing," said Sheriff Brown, handing the pack to John.

Corky and Jinx jumped out of the van and came to John. He let them sniff the fanny pack.

"Have everyone stop what they are doing and let the dogs work," said John.

Sheriff Brown picked up his bullhorn and clicked the trigger. "Everyone stop where you are. Freeze."

"Find," said John, holding the little pack so the dogs could sniff it again. He put on his backpack from the van and patiently waited.

Both dogs circled the campground, running up and back on the various trails. Jinx went to the dirt road going up the mountain and sat down. Zeke walked over and stood by the dog for a moment. Zeke and Jinx moved up the trail.

"Come on, Riley. Corky has the little girl's scent," said Lila. The two girls hurried over to follow Zeke and Jinx up the mountain trail.

Jinx led the group running up the trail, followed by Chet and Roy. The dogs were soon out of sight.

"Sheriff, the dogs have the girl's scent. Zeke will mark a trail for us to follow," said John, keying his walkie-talkie.

"Keep me posted," said the voice of Sheriff Brown.

***

A TV van pulled up, and its crew began setting up equipment to transmit the story to their waiting audience.

A female deputy talked to the girl's tearful parents, while the J Bar J rescue team followed dog tracks up the trail.

Zeke ran thirty yards behind the dogs, often with the dogs out of sight. Corky ran to a stump, sniffed for several seconds, and went into search mode.

Jinx reached the stump and began barking. Zeke reached the stump and read the signs in the dirt. "Bear track, John. It's walking with the girl."

"How big?"

"A two-legged bear, walking upright like a man," said Zeke.

***

John keyed his walkie-talkie. "Sheriff, Zeke says a two-legged bear is walking with the girl."

"A two-legged bear? What does he mean?"

"A person wearing bear paws tied to his or her feet," said John.

"What do you make of it?" asked the sheriff.

"It's an attempt to disguise the tracks," said John. He hurried up the trail toward Overlook Point.

***

Corky and Jinx reached the cliffs overlooking the long valley. They lay down.

Lila and Riley ran up, panting, and joined them.

"Now we wait," said Lila, taking deep breaths.

A tall young man reached out of the bushes and grabbed Riley by his left hand.

"Hey, quit it," screamed Riley.

Corky leaped and clamped his teeth on the man's arm.

"Oww!" yelled the young man, hitting the dog's nose with his right hand. Corky let go and stood between Riley and the man in the bushes.

"Riley, pet Corky," said Lila, concerned.

Riley reached over and stroked the dog's head. "Good Corky."

"Looks like he got away," Lila noted.

Zeke ran up and joined them. "What happened?"

"Somebody grabbed me," said Riley.

"John," said Zeke into this walkie-talkie.

"Go ahead, Zeke," said John.

"A man attacked Lila and Riley. Corky drove him off. The trail ends at the cliffs at Lookout Point."

"Who was the attacker?"

"It was Chip," said Lila.

"Zeke, Lila, and Riley, search the cliff area. John out."

Zeke glanced at Riley. "You wear the airplane pack instead of the mountain pack? Why?"

Lila laughed. "You picked up the wrong pack."

"Oh," said Riley, turning red with embarrassment.

Zeke and Jinx moved right along the cliff.

"Corky, come. Let's go left," said Lila.

The two girls moved along a dim path that circled the rim of the canyon. They heard a faint voice. "I don't want to," said a child.

"Oh, come on. It'll be fun," whispered a male voice.

Riley and Lila stepped into an open area.

A man stood with a hang glider strapped to his back. A young girl slapped the man's hands, screamed, and pulled back. She fell against Riley. Looking up, the girl jumped, wrapped her arms around her neck, and clamped her legs around her waist.

Surprised, Riley held the girl. "I'm Riley. I'm your friend. You're safe."

Corky growled and moved between Riley and the man.

The man spun around. His glider wing knocked Lila to the ground. Corky jumped out of the way. Stepping forward, the man spun the glider, hitting Riley in the back. Pushing off, the man caused Riley and the little girl to fall off the cliff.

Corky raced to the cliff edge and barked.

"Oh no! John!" Lila called on her shoulder comm unit.

"John here."

"Riley and a little girl were pushed off the cliff by a man in a hang glider."

"Do you see them?"

"No. They've disappeared."

***

Falling, the girl screamed in Riley's ear and held on for dear life.

Riley's feet bounced against the cliff. She stepped twice on the vertical cliff and then jumped away from the solid rock.

"Hang on," Riley whispered in her ear in an attempt to calm her. She reached up, grabbed the handles on the jacket shoulders, and pulled as hard as she could. She locked her hands behind the girl, just before the parachute popped open.

The girl screamed and held on tighter.

"Riley, concentrate," said Lila's voice.

Riley got a determined look on her face.

"Shhh, it's okay. I'm Riley. What's your name?"

"Sherry. Hold me. I'm scared."

"Just hold tight. We have help," Riley said.

"And a parachute," said Sherry, looking up.

"Riley, steer away from the cliff. Head down the valley," said John's voice.

"How?" asked a calming Riley.

"Reach up to the parachute lines. Pull one side and then the other. You will glide away from the cliff," John instructed.

"I can't. I'm holding a little girl," said Riley, clutching onto Sherry.

"Riley, I see you in my binoculars. Use one arm and follow the hang glider heading down the valley."

"What is going on? I'm rising." Riley reached up and gently pulled at the shrouds.

"The sun has heated the air near the cliffs. Heat rises. As you move down the valley, you will drop," said John.

"I thought parachute training was in two weeks."

"Surprise," said John. "You know my motto."

"Be ready for the unexpected."

"Riley," said Sherry, clinging, frightened, but excited.

"Yes, Sherry?"

"My mom is going to be real surprised I got to take a parachute ride."

"Ditto," said Riley, trying to stop shaking, as they floated down the valley.

***

"Sheriff, this is John."

"Go ahead, John. I've monitored your situation."

John walked down the trail until he met the sheriff. "The trail ends at Lookout Point."

"Oh no, not another kid falling off that cliff," said Sheriff Brown.

"Another?"

"Do you remember eight weeks ago when the Anderson kid disappeared? She fell near there."

"As I recall, no body was found," said John.

"We'll find her someday in the rough terrain," said the sheriff.

The walkie-talkie broke in. "John?"

"Yes, Zeke?"

"I suggest you blockade the canyon with hundred-yard intercept."

John turned to the sheriff. "May I suggest you close the canyon and check every vehicle for the missing children?"

"Agreed," said the sheriff.

"Further, I suggest a hundred-yard intercept if anyone tries to turn around at the roadblock," said John in his sternest voice. "Plus, use all camcorders and dashboard cameras."

"John, you're serious?"

"There is no time to lose."

The sheriff pulled out his cell phone and dialed. "This is Brown. Set up roadblocks on both ends of the Lake Fork Canyon. Set a car at a hundred yards back up the road from each roadblock in case anyone tries to escape. Turn on all dash cams." He hung up. "Satisfied?"

John smiled.

"This one may cost you some Police Ball tickets, John," said the sheriff with a smile.

"You said to find the children," replied John.

The phone buzzed. The sheriff picked it up and listened. "A second child, Angie Ledbetter, age six, is also missing," he said.

"In this area?"

"Yes." Sheriff Brown dialed his phone to relay the information. "Check every car."

***

Lila sat waiting at Lookout Point, when movement attracted her attention.

"Is that a hang glider just rising out of the trees?"

"Yes," said Zeke.

Their shoulder comm units clicked on. "This is John. Look for any activity and report."

Lila clicked on her comm unit. "John, another hang glider just appeared below Lookout Point."

John's voice came over the walkie-talkie. "Sheriff Brown and J Bar J team, watch for more hang gliders and report at once."

***

Deputy Sheriff Lance Philips stopped just before coming to a sharp curve in the winding road. His partner, Deputy Ed Rilling, drove up the road and backed his patrol car out of sight around the curve.

Philips's patrol car blocked the road, making it necessary for all cars to stop. He activated the dash camera.

A four-wheel-drive truck came around the curve with a hang glider strapped on its rack. Brakes squealed. The truck stopped, reversed, and immediately backed into a patrol car that appeared out of nowhere, causing a crease in the patrol car's fender and hood.

The driver put the truck in park, jumped out of the cab, and ran into the foliage on the mountainside, disappearing up the hill.

Deputy Sheriff Rilling approached the driver's open door. Inside sat a six-year-old girl.

"Hi, I'm Angie Ledbetter. What's your name?" she asked.

The deputy keyed the microphone on his shoulder. "Sheriff, this is Phillips. We just found the Ledbetter girl. She was in a truck with a hang glider. The male driver escaped into the bushes."

"Tell me you had the dash camera operating," said Brown.

"Yes, sir, just as you ordered. I'll flash send a photo of the driver to all units."

"Sheriff Brown to all units. Report all hang-gliding activities at once."

John activated his comm unit. "All searchers watch for hang gliders. Report any sightings."

"John, this is Lila. A hang glider just took flight off the cliffs southeast of our position."

"Where is it headed?" asked John.

"Just in circles. It has a female adult and a Hispanic child—a girl," responded Lila, looking through her binoculars.

"Sheriff, John here. We've spotted the kidnappers of Tina Rodriguez. All searchers get to higher ground, use binoculars, and find out where the hang glider lands."

"John, this is Zeke. Did you say kidnappers?"

"Yes, kidnappers."

"Zeke again. There are only three places they can land in this canyon. The largest one is at Oak Creek campground. There is a large soccer field there."

"John, this is Sheriff Brown. I'll send my fast-response team to the soccer field at the Oak Creek campground."

"Okay, Sheriff. Riley and a little girl parachuted down the valley," said John.

"Parachuted? I'll pass the word. Brown out."

***

Sheriff's cars and vans raced, sirens screaming, into the soccer field just in time to apprehend a woman, about thirty, as she landed her hang glider on the field.

When the deputies surrounded the woman, the little girl exclaimed, "Oh, Andi, that was fun. You were right. But why are all these policemen here?"

The deputies put the woman into a squad car; she refused to give any information. The deputies detained a second man when a white van tried to leave the soccer field.

***

"Riley, you will reach the soccer field shortly. There is plenty of room to land," John alerted her over the radio.

"How do we land?"

"Standing up. Pretend to run. Just before you touch the ground, keep running."

"Great. How many lessons are there for your parachute class?" asked Riley.

"Three. Parachute packing, muscle training, and the jump," said John.

"Nice. I think I'll just skip to the jumping part."

Lila's laughter came over the comm link.

"John, I see the jerk who pushed me off the cliff with his hang glider. He landed in a small field on the side of the mountain. It looks like he's putting his glider on a jeep," said Riley.

"Roger. John to Sheriff."

"I heard her, John. I'll check into it. Sheriff out."

***

Near a bridge under repair, another four-wheel-drive truck with a tied-down hang glider slid to a stop. Thirty feet away, a police officer talked with a couple waiting impatiently for repairs to the road to get done so they could leave the canyon.

The driver of the truck watched the three talk for a moment; glancing in her rear-view mirror, she was stunned to see a police car parked just off the road in the bushes.

She shut off her engine, got out of the truck, and walked toward the area where heavy equipment had just placed two large pipes in the stream to keep it flowing. A bulldozer dug into the hillside and pushed fill dirt over the pipes, so the water could continue running down the stream.

It was going to be hours before anyone could leave the canyon. The woman walked upstream a short distance, crossed the running water, and climbed onto a dirt road. She walked out of sight up the canyon.

The policeman walked up to the truck and peeked inside. "Who are you?" he asked the young girl sitting on the seat.

"I'm Jennifer."

The policeman activated his shoulder microphone. "Sheriff Brown, do we have any more missing kids?"

"This is Brown. We received notice a Jennifer Lowe is missing."

"This is Officer Widdison at Blue Fork Bridge. Jennifer Lowe was just found at this location in a four-wheeler with a hang glider."

***

Zeke and Spic continued along the rim. A short distance from the top of the ridge, a young man dressed in camouflage hiking gear jumped out of the bushes. He ran directly at the cliff and jumped into space.

"John, a hiker ran from Spic and leaped off the cliff," said Lila's voice. "He's wearing a parachute."

"Zeke, Lila, use your binoculars. You have one minute to give me a location where the parachutist lands," John replied.

The two pulled out their binoculars, focused on the parachute, activated their recorders, and followed him down to a road.

"John, the parachutist landed on the dirt road off Highway 3310," said Zeke.

"John, this is Lila. A second parachutist landed at the same spot. We've lost sight of them among the trees."

John's walkie-talkie clicked on. "Clear. See Slim."

***

The hang glider dropped onto the soccer field. The man ran a few steps and stopped. He was surrounded by police and put into handcuffs.

"Gangway," yelled Riley, dropping quickly to the ground.

"Look out! A parachutist," yelled a police officer.

Riley started running just before she touched the ground. She ran, stumbled, ran for nearly thirty feet, and then stopped.

"Okay, Sherry. We're down," said Riley.

"Can we do it again? That was fun," said Sherry, dropping to the ground.

Riley breathed a sigh of relief. "Not today," she said, starting to shake.

The two girls were quickly surrounded by police.

"Sheriff, this is Officer Corn at the soccer field. We have two more arrivals."

"Ask them their names," said the sheriff.

"What are your names?" asked Officer Corn.

"Riley."

"Sherry."

"Officer Corn, the parachutist, Riley, is part of John Johnson's team. John will pick her up. The girl, Sherry, will go with you to the station," said the sheriff's voice.

"Roger, Sheriff."

Riley began folding her parachute.

***

At the J Bar J, John hung up the phone and turned to his staff. "The sheriff said he hit a dead end. The vehicles and hang gliders were stolen. All three kids told the same story: they went for a walk, met a person, went to find Mom and Dad, walked to a cliff, got on the hang glider, frightened, but loved it. The woman and man caught at the ball field refuse to say anything at all."

"A pretty fancy kidnapping plan," said Betty.

"Very ingenious," said Chet.

Zeke nodded. "No tracks in air."

"And Riley got her first parachute lesson," said Lila.

"Thanks, I think," said Riley.

Laughter filled the room.

"There are five children, ages six to ten, missing from this area over the past three years," said John. "I fear we will never find them."

CHAPTER 4

Riley's Distraction

If your life is drudgery, climb Inspiration Hill
and leave your burdens for the wind to blow away.
—Sensei J.R. Jensen

At the J Bar J, Donna answered the insistent phone.

"May I speak with my daughter?" asked a female voice.

"Who is your daughter?"

"Riley Whirl."

"One minute." Donna pressed the wall buzzer six times.

In their room, Lila counted the buzzes. "It's for one of us. Come on, down to the kitchen phone."

The two girls safely raced to the kitchen.

"Who is it for?" asked Lila.

"Riley," said Donna, handing her the phone.

"This is Riley."

"Oh, Riley, this is Mom. Dad had a nervous breakdown. I'm going to have to try and find a job. He is okay now but must stay in the hospital for several days."

"Is there something I can do?" asked Riley, concerned.

Lila stood close enough to hear the conversation.

"No, your brother got a job, so we'll be okay as soon as I get working," said Mom. "I love you. I'll call in about a week."

"Okay, Mom, I love you too."

"Unwelcome news?" asked Lila.

"Yes, Dad had a nervous breakdown with the stress of no job."

Lila took Riley by the hand. "Let's talk to John."

John's office door stood open, and John sat at his desk. When the two girls appeared in his doorway, he waved them inside. "What brings you two to my door?" he asked, looking first at one girl and then the other.

Riley sighed. "It's my dad. He had a nervous breakdown with all the stresses at home and no job."

"What kind of stress?"

"Well, Dad lost his job when the plant closed, and all the jobs were sent overseas. Then, with no money coming in, we lost the house and had to move into Grandpa and Grandma's house. My coming here made more room for those left behind and helped on food too."

"Go on," said John.

"So, Mom is looking for a job to pay the bills. My brother, Terry, is working, but I don't know what he's doing."

John rubbed his chin. "After dinner, call your brother and find out what is going on."

***

At his grandpa and grandma's house, Terry answered the phone.

"Terry, it's good to hear your voice."

"Riley. How is life at Uncle John's dude ranch?"

"It's busy. I'm getting more training to join his ghost recon team. But my reason for calling is to find out about Dad."

"Well, he had a nervous breakdown yesterday. The doctor put him in the hospital. Thank goodness we still have our medical and dental insurance," he said.

"With Dad out of work, how can you afford it?"

"I got my old job back. I use most of my paycheck to pay the medical premiums."

"Where do you work?"

"I'm back at Skinny Minnie's hot dogs."

"How is Grandma doing?"

"She's in a wheelchair now, and the doctor has her taking twenty different pills a day. We pay the bills, and what is left we use for the food budget."

"Terry, get Dad's bank book account and direct deposit number. I'm getting a paycheck. I'll send money to help the cause," said Riley.

"Sis, that would really help. Just a minute." Shortly, Terry had the bank numbers for Riley, and she wrote them on a card.

"I better go," said Riley.

"Thanks for the extra money. We can sure use it. Bye."

Riley hung up the phone.

"Where does your brother work?" asked John, seated at his desk.

"At Skinny Minnie's hot dogs," said Riley with a laugh. She took a bite of toast and sat in her chair, chewing and staring into space.

"Staff, Riley seems distracted. Does anyone have an idea?" asked John.

"Perhaps Riley could tell us her distraction," said Donna.

Riley sighed. "My family is going through a tough time with Dad out of work and my grandmother ill."

"What can you do to help them?" asked Zeke.

"I'll send my salary to them."

"All of it?" asked John.

"Yes. Here are the bank account numbers." Riley passed the numbers to John.

John handed the sheet of paper to Donna. "Include articles fourteen and twenty-seven with Riley's salary."

"What are articles fourteen and twenty-seven?" asked Riley.

"Article fourteen gives us permission to contact former employers. Article twenty-seven has two parts: a bonus given by the police and our friends to the ghost recon team for catching criminals with bounties on their heads. Each team member receives a portion of the bounties. It's like a savings account," said John.

"Oh, thank you. It will really help." Riley squinted in thought.

"Part two is a bonus. The amount of money in your article twenty-seven is twelve thousand dollars," said Donna.

Riley's mouth dropped open. "What? Where did the money come from?"

"The standard reward for preventing a kidnapping is three thousand dollars for each team member for each child. We saved three kids," said Zeke.

"Riley got an extra three thousand dollars for her parachute jump," said Lila.

Laughter filled the room.

"That money will get me to the university this fall," said Riley, obviously pleased.

"Donna, prepare a picnic lunch. Take it to Inspiration Hill at 10:30 in the morning," said John.

***

The J Bar J van pulled up and stopped at the base of Inspiration Hill. The team of John, Lila, Riley, Zeke, and Nathan got out and walked to the covered pavilion.

"Everyone pick up a backpack from the first table. On each of the tables are rocks painted with words like *discouraged, angry,* or *sad.* Pick up the rocks that pertain to you and place them in your backpack," said John.

Riley walked around and picked up rocks from nearly every table. She picked up *sad, discouraged, angry, no money,* and *in the dumps.* She hefted her pack; it was heavy.

Lila walked behind her and commented, "You have a lot of distractions."

"Distractions?"

"Distractions slow us down. Our team cannot do its job with any distractions."

"Everyone take a seat by the fireplace. Sit an arm's length apart. Keep silent," said John.

The team sat by the glowing fireplace, putting their backpacks beside them. Firelight reflected off their faces.

"Everyone close your eyes. Imagine you are in a park on a mountain."

"But that is where we are," Riley whispered to Lila.

"You are correct," Lila whispered back to her roommate, her eyes closed.

Riley closed her eyes.

"Imagine a trail that goes up the mountain. You are hiking on this trail. Ahead is a path separation. One path continues up, and the other path drops down. I want you to pick the path going up," said John.

The team sat by the fireplace with their eyes closed.

"Take ten imaginary steps and stop. Now open your eyes and take out the rock from your pack with the word you feel is weighing you down the most."

Riley opened her eyes, opened her pack, and reached in. She paused and then pulled out *discouragement*.

"Drop the rock on the ground," said John.

Riley let the rock fall. *Discouragement* landed with a thud.

"Now let the wind blow away the name on your rock. You now feel lighter," said John. "With your eyes closed, hike up the path again."

The team sat with eyes closed.

"On a tree branch, a bird sits in its nest. It has blue feathers. On the ground before you, a small bird flaps and jumps around. With your mind's eye, pick up the baby bird and place it back in its nest."

Riley, eyes closed, mentally picked up the baby bird and placed it back in its nest.

"The mother bird pecks your hand," said John.

Lila reached over and pricked Riley's hand with a needle.

"Ouch!" cried Riley, confused.

"Keep your eyes closed and repeat after me," said John.

Riley held her eyelids together.

"I picked up the baby bird," said John.

"I picked up the baby bird," said the group.

"The mother bird pecked my hand," said John.

"The mother bird pecked my hand," said the group.

"The mother bird was protecting her baby," said John.

"The mother bird was protecting her baby," said the group.

"We protect the innocent, helpless, and deserving," said John.

"We protect the innocent, helpless, and deserving," said the group.

"Riley, open your eyes," said John.

Riley opened her eyes. The back of her hand was bleeding. Lila pulled out a Band-Aid and put it on the injury.

"If you wish to protect the innocent, helpless, and deserving, please stand," said John.

The entire group, including Riley, stood.

"Pick up your packs and follow me." John walked up the trail toward the top of the hill.

Lila helped Riley put on her pack.

"Why was I hurt?" whispered Riley.

"The work we do can be, and is, dangerous. John always says be ready for any eventuality, even being hurt," whispered Lila.

"So?"

"Let's walk up the trail."

The two girls followed the group up the trail. One hundred yards up the trail was another small pavilion. The group sat on the ground around a blazing fire pit.

"Sit and close your eyes. Think, then pull out the next stone with its name and drop it on the ground," said John.

Riley sat and thought. She pulled out the rock *sad*, dropping it on the ground.

For the next hour, the group walked, stopped, sat thinking, and dropped rocks onto the ground.

At the top of the hill, John instructed the group to sit around a prepared fire pit. He lit the fire.

Donna was there with the picnic lunch. "Come get it," she said.

The group walked over to the food and picked up plates, forks, and cups. They filled their plates and began eating.

As they ate, John walked around, handing cards to each person.

Riley looked at the cards John gave her: *protect, happy, talents, care for others,* and *concerned.*

"Everyone, open your packs and pull out any rocks that are left."

Riley pulled out her lone rock. It said "no money."

"Riley is the only one who has a rock. It says *no money.* What do we do about that?" John asked.

"Give me some money?" asked Riley.

The group laughed.

"Lila, tell her our secret," said John, sitting down with a plate of food. He began to eat.

Lila pulled a thin purse from her pack and handed it to Riley.

"You have dropped all your worries and distractions on the mountain. This purse has a credit card and ten twenty-dollar bills. Now you have money, since you sent all your bank money to your family," she said.

Riley looked at John with a question in her eyes.

"You have left all distractions on the hill. The credit card and cash are to let you know I trust you. You are a member of the team."

Lila whispered in Riley's ear. "All distractions are gone. Your family is taken care of, and now you can concentrate on the training and missions."

Riley's eyes brimmed with tears as if a great weight had been lifted from her shoulders.

***

Riley looked at the bulletin board outside her room. Staring back at her was her photo.

"What does this mean?" Riley asked Lila, showing her the photo.

"Run down to John's office. Go now."

Riley ran downstairs and entered John's office. He handed her a set of papers. The heading said, "State University."

"Fill them out right now. We have more to do," said John, handing her a pen.

Riley sat and began filling out the papers. "I need to send a registration fee."

"Donna has the check already filled out. Hand her the papers on your way back up to your room."

Later, Riley finished the papers and walked into the kitchen.

Donna held out her hand. "This will go out in today's mail."

CHAPTER 5

Jake Logan

When capture is imminent,
you have one second to escape.
—Sensei J. R. Jensen

Jake Logan sat in his plush red chair, hands folded. Six young men sat on hard chairs.

"The hang gliding program is dead," said Jake.

Nobody said a word.

"We need five more kids to fill the contract. Then we move operations."

"What plan, boss?" asked Herman, leader of the skinhead group.

"Use the playground cleanup gag," said Jake.

***

At Liberty Park Elementary School, a large, white, unmarked van pulled up to the curb. The driver stayed in the driver's seat, engine running. Five men dressed in work overalls got out of the van with large plastic garbage bags and began picking up trash on the playground.

Miss Lark Ellington brought her fifth-grade class to the softball diamond to play kickball. Miss Ellington blew her whistle. "Cami and Liz are captains." The girls picked their teams, and play began.

The five men stopped to watch. Suddenly, the tall man with big ears rushed over and sprayed a mist in the teacher's face and the faces of five girls. Miss Ellington collapsed. Five girls slumped to the ground. The other children ran screaming toward the school.

The five men lifted the five unconscious girls through the side door into the van, climbed in, and the van drove away.

Three minutes later and two blocks away, the van drove up a ramp onto a semi-truck parked on a side street. The driver closed and locked the rear door. The truck drove to the nearby interstate highway and turned south.

***

Within fifteen minutes, police issued an Amber Alert; roadblocks were set up all around the city. All large white vans were stopped and searched, but the five girls had simply disappeared. Parents were in tears at the loss of their daughters.

The news media issued on-the-spot reports at the school.

The FBI entered the case.

Psychologists visited Miss Ellington's class to provide comfort and counseling to the upset children.

***

John sat on his favorite chair, deep in thought; he pressed the intercom button and said, "Zeke, meet me at the jeep."

Zeke hurried to the jeep.

"We received a short message," said John.

"Did our spy tell us about the kidnappings?" asked Zeke.

"He did. He said Slim."

"Let's go see our old friend Slim," said Zeke.

The jeep sped out of J Bar J and drove to a rundown neighborhood. John and Zeke entered a basement apartment in the quiet slum.

Gently, John shook Slim Ziker awake. Slim yawned and sat up.

"No lights," said John.

"Hi, John. Zeke," said Slim.

"You are going to the races today, Slim," said John.

"I can't. Logan is lookin' for me."

"After you pay Logan, you will take a vacation."

"What's the catch?"

"With Logan paid, you'll want to visit Hawaii," whispered John.

"Yeah? I want a hundred thousand dollars," said Slim, catching on quickly.

John just smiled in the dim light. "Six thousand for gambling debts, plus ten thousand dollars and a plane ticket."

Slim was silent. "It's those Elementary kids, isn't it?"

"Where are they?" asked John.

Slim remained silent.

"You owe me big time, Slim."

Slim gave a great sigh, as if surrendering. "Logan has a friend on the Texas-Mexico border. He likes very young ladies to work free in his vineyards.

"Where?"

"The Mexican border near river bend. The guy is Tito Munge," said Slim.

"Zeke will accompany you to the races. He has two envelopes. One has your debt payment and the other your travel money and plane ticket. Have a nice month vacation trip."

CHAPTER 6

—

Mexico Trip

Know your enemy's strengths.
Now use them against him (her).
—Sensei J. R. Jensen

Daily News Bulletin. Brownsville, Texas. The FBI, Immigration and Naturalization Service, Texas Rangers, and local police raided the Munge Vineyards. Police officers detained and deported forty illegal aliens. A judge ordered Munge to pay a $1,800 fine. The fine was paid, and Munge crossed the border into Mexico.

***

"Someone warned Munge. It means we have to take a trip to Mexico," said John, putting down the newspaper.

"As illegal aliens?" asked Zeke with his normal unemotional face.

Lila smothered a laugh.

John snorted. "We'll get in and out in disguises. Those kidnapped girls must come home."

"What is the plan?" asked Chet.

"Three days from today, we go to the Mexican border. Zeke found the five missing girls from Liberty Park Elementary at the

Munge Vineyards on the Mexican side of the border," said John. "Zeke."

Zeke nodded. "The girls work in pairs. Each pair has one older girl and one younger girl. We have identified the older girls. They were kidnapped from the George Washington Elementary school ten days ago. The FBI failed to find them because someone warned Munge, and they were moved to his Mexican vineyards."

John put color photos of the girls on the table. "Memorize the photos of these girls." He held up a photo. "This is Cami. She is thin and tall like Riley. We plan to disguise Riley and switch her and Cami, then rescue any girls we can find in the vineyard."

"Any girls?" asked Chet.

"There could be other kidnapped girls in the nearby vineyards," said Zeke.

Roy raised his hand. "What is our assignment?"

"Stealth in, stealth out," replied John.

***

The following two days of training sped by in a neighborhood vineyard. All aspects of fieldwork were covered: dress, manners, and how to pick the grapes. The team studied Spanish vocabulary every spare minute while training in a terrain similar to Munge's vineyard.

On the second day, John called Riley into his office. "Please shut the door and sit down," he said.

Riley did as she was told.

"I'm pleased to see you are very proficient with all levels I taught you," he said.

"Terry and I worked on our techniques every day since you moved. I needed a partner, and he was willing to keep up his skills." Riley settled into a comfortable beanbag chair.

"As this is your third operation with the team, I'll have you stick close to Lila. She is quick and efficient. Further, you will be expected to act if the need arises."

"Expect the unexpected?" asked Riley.

"Exactly. Just like your parachute jump."

The door opened, and Lila, Betty, Chet, and Roy entered and sat down.

"Riley will be traded for the tallest girl, Cami, tomorrow just after they begin picking grapes," said John.

"Is she ready?" asked Betty.

"She is. The harvest is nearly over, and the girls will soon be moved."

"Where?" asked Chet.

"We don't know. If they are moved, we've lost them. Girls, wear the desert packs," said John.

***

Early on the third day, a group of elderly tourists got into a white bus, with Riley sitting in the front seat, close to the driver.

"It's nice to be myself," Riley said in her blouse and knee-length pants. A thin pack was on her back. Her right cheek was covered by makeup, to cover her burn scars.

The nice little old lady in the seat behind her just smiled. "I'll put on your makeup to look like that kidnapped girl, Cami, just before we reach the vineyard," said Lila's voice.

The bus headed south with Corky curled up and asleep on the back seat.

CHAPTER 7

The Vineyard

Train your feet to move smoothly,
silently in every terrain.
—Sensei J. R. Jensen

Before sunup, the van pulled into a motel and restaurant complex. After breakfast, the van drove down a dusty road and turned around at a river's edge.

Zeke waited for the van, dressed in camouflage clothing. He motioned for the team to don backpacks and follow him.

"No light, no noise, no fire," he whispered.

The team followed Zeke across the landscape, crossed a river in canoes, and moved into an irrigation ditch next to a vineyard.

As they approached, they saw the kidnapped girls picking grapes, closely watched by other field workers.

The team watched until Cami walked around the end row. Zeke and Chet appeared at her side. Chet covered her mouth, so she couldn't cry out and pulled her swiftly to the ground. "Cami, we are friends. We are here to rescue you. I'm going to let go of your mouth. Can you be quiet?"

Cami nodded and relaxed.

Zeke covered her with a camouflage sheet and had her crawl out of sight into the irrigation ditch.

Riley walked over and took her place, picking grapes, dressed in vineyard clothing and sandals and carrying a basket.

Zeke appeared and covered the second girl's mouth when she reached the end of the row. "Liz, keep quiet."

At the irrigation ditch, Cami stood and touched her finger to her mouth. Liz blinked and relaxed.

Chet helped Liz step into the irrigation ditch to hide.

Zeke moved down the row behind Riley. He seemed to disappear.

Lila joined Chet and the girls in the irrigation ditch.

In a very soft voice, Lila asked, "Danger?"

"The dogs," whispered Liz, obviously frightened.

"How are they dangerous?" asked Chet.

"When we go to eat, the dogs sniff us," said Liz.

"And?"

"Your lady would be attacked immediately" Cami said softly.

Zeke placed his hand by his mouth and whistled like a dove.

Riley looked toward the sound and nodded slightly. She took the grapes and gently placed them in a nearby wooden box. The box was nearly full of grapes.

A small girl walked up and placed grapes into the wooden box, filling it up. She blinked twice when she saw Riley. "Who are you?"

Zeke appeared out of nowhere and covered the girl's mouth.

"I'm Riley. We're here to rescue you."

"Don't scream when I release your mouth," said Zeke.

The startled girl nodded, and Zeke released her.

"Who are you?" asked Riley.

"I'm Danni Anderson," she said. "Where are Cami, Liz, and Clara?"

"Cami and Liz are nearby, watching us. They're with friends," whispered Riley. "Who is Clara?"

"She works two rows over."

Zeke disappeared into the foliage. He moved swiftly two rows over and began picking grapes next to Clara, putting the grapes in her holder.

"You are new. What do you want?" whispered Clara.

"Cami, Liz, and Danni are going home with friends. Would you like to go too?"

"Home? Can the ten other girls go with us?" asked Clara.

"Ten girls? No, we must leave at once."

"Then I must stay and protect the younger girls."

"I'm sorry. I'll return, but now I must leave you." Zeke hid a small barrette in her hair and slipped away into the foliage just before a massive male worker walked up, picked up the full wooden box of grapes, and walked away.

***

"Riley, pick faster," whispered Danni. "We must have another full box ready when he returns, or we get whipped."

"Continue picking," said Riley. The two girls picked until they reached the end of the row. They filled a box just as the husky man approached. He picked up the full box and left.

Riley grabbed Danni's hand. "Follow me."

***

Not far away, a van coughed, blew smoke, and started to move. It stopped rolling at the Munge Vineyard road turnoff. The van's driver and four old, angry men and women climbed down and hobbled into the main yard. Several dogs raced out and barked at the group. One dog tried to bite, but one old fellow bent over and sprayed the dog in the face. The dog ran away howling. A distinctly skunky smell filled the air.

Munge appeared on the front porch. He saw the old people, reached over, and rang a bell. The sound carried all over the vineyard.

Immediately, workers stopped what they were doing and ran toward a shed near the house.

Riley and Danni ran away from the house.

Munge saw them and whistled. Four dogs raced after the girls.

Riley directed the girl to the road, where a white van waited.

"Quickly, into the van." Riley and Danni entered the van.

Spic growled at the dogs.

The van door slid shut with a distinct bang.

Chet sprayed the air over the top of the van. The Munge dogs raced away howling.

"Don't open the door. We have a skunk nearby." Chet laughed.

"Cami, Liz, we're safe," said Danni. The three girls laughed, cried, and hugged.

"We must leave. Grab a seat," said Chet.

The girls sat together on the same bench seat, chattering as the van sped away.

"Seat belts," said Chet.

"Danni, we're on our way home," said Cami.

"Where is Zeke?" asked Riley.

Lila just winked and settled down for the ride home.

***

The old people tottered and caned up to the porch. A young girl opened the screen door and stopped.

"Get off my property!" yelled Munge.

"What a pretty little girl," said an old man.

"What is your name?" asked an aged woman.

"This is my daughter, Sela," interrupted Munge.

"Are all these girls your daughters?" asked an old lady.

A police car arrived, lights flashing. The officer got out of the car and approached the group.

"What is the problem, Señor Munge?"

"Just some trespassers who are leaving," replied Munge.

"You must leave," said the officer, directing his words to the old folks.

"Okay, everyone get back in the van. Let's go," said the driver.

"Would you sell this little girl to me?" asked the old man.

"Sell my daughter?" asked Munge.

"I have need for her, say a thousand dollars?"

Munge thought a moment. "Cash," he said.

The old man excitedly handed him an envelope.

Munge opened the envelope, counted the money, and nodded.

"Go with the nice man, Sela," said Munge.

The police officer walked over to Munge, shook hands, and received a hundred-dollar bill. He escorted the old people with Sela back to their van; then he climbed into his police car and drove away.

***

A laborer ran to Munge and whispered, "A van escapes with three slaves. They speed to the river."

Munge watched two white vans disappear down the road. He rang the porch bell three times. A maid brought him a full glass of lemonade. He sipped the drink and watched the furious activity.

A laborer ran over to the slave cottage and pulled open the door. "All outside."

Eleven white girls hurried outside. Each girl carried a blanket, a bottle of water, and a see-through plastic bag filled with a comb, wash rag, bar of soap, and toothbrush.

A pickup truck and two jeeps appeared and screeched to a halt in front of the girls, who got into the truck, sitting along each side. One girl sat with her back to the cab.

Munge walked over to the truck driver. "Take them to Farm Alpha. Give them hoes, and put them to work. Bring the Mexican girls back to this farm at once."

The three vehicles sped south, leaving behind a cloud of dust.

***

Zeke sprinted south on the dusty road, away from the Munge farm. "John, I planted a global positioning device on Clara. Link my phone to the satellite. I need to know where they are taking her, because she stayed behind to protect ten younger girls."

The two jeeps and the pickup headed in Zeke's direction. He stepped into the brush beside the road. The vehicles sped down the road, and dust blanketed the brush.

"John here. You have your satellite link. Good luck."

Zeke stepped out of the brush and jogged south. "Indio, India, and Puma, converge on the satellite signal. We will need two or three pickups."

***

At Munge Farm Alpha, the vehicles drove into the farmyard; dust followed them and settled on everything in sight. The head peon walked to the porch and rang the bell four times.

Female Mexican workers ran from the fields and waited by the porch. The white girls were ordered out of the pickup, handed hoes, and guided by a worker into the fields.

Clara pantomimed that she needed water and pointed to the other girls. An older Mexican lady nodded.

The Mexican girls climbed into the pickup, which raced out of the farmyard, followed by the two jeeps, heading back the way they had come.

***

In the field, a peon showed the girls how to hoe the rows of corn. He watched each girl until he was satisfied the slave labor knew what to do.

Soon, the old Mexican lady walked to each girl and handed her a bottle of water.

"Thank you," said Clara.

"You will be summoned after the evening meal. Be ready."

"What does that mean?" asked Clara.

"You will be assigned living space," she said and walked away.

Clara continued to hoe. She glanced up and saw an Aztec girl standing at the end of her row. The Indian girl motioned for her to come.

As Clara neared the girl, three pickup trucks skidded to a stop on the dirt road behind her, dust flying.

Zeke jumped out of one pickup. "Clara, do you remember me?"

"Yes. You said you would see me again soon."

"How do you call the girls together?"

Clara put her fingers in her mouth and whistled. Immediately, ten girls surrounded her.

"Clara and one girl, come with me. India, take five girls with you. Indio, take four girls with you. Get in the pickups. We are going home to the United States."

The girls squealed in relief and delight.

The pickups quickly filled and sped north toward the border.

***

"John, this is Zeke. We are nearing the river at the assigned location with eleven girls. What are your instructions?"

"Zeke, tell me what you see."

"Wow. I see two military helicopters landing in front of us."

John laughed over the comm system. "Have a nice flight home."

The girls began cheering.

"I think the girls heard you, John," said Zeke.

"On behalf of the girls, I thank you," said Clara, seated next to Zeke in the lead pickup truck. Tears welled up in her eyes as overwhelming gratitude flooded her emotions.

"Team, abandon the pickups and get into the choppers. Let's get out of here," said Zeke.

The team and the girls climbed into the helicopters, strapped in, and held on for the ride to American soil.

As the helicopters lifted off, three men emerged from the bushes near the river. They walked to the pickups, started them, and drove away.

A jeep appeared, and the driver got out. He made a circle with his right thumb and pointer finger and placed it against the palm of his left hand.

"John, this is Zeke. Jose gave the 'fly safe' sign."

"I'll thank him when I see him," replied John.

***

The entire rescue team stood with John on the front porch of the J Bar J ranch house.

"I wanted you all to be here when we receive our next visitors," said John.

A stretch limousine drove up to the house. The door opened, and Danni jumped out and ran to Riley. She hugged Riley as hard as she could.

"We thank you," wept the mother, stepping out of the limo.

"John," said the father, handing him a briefcase, "here is positive action for the work you do."

"Thanks, we'll use it well," said John.

Lila looked at Riley. "Those parents really love their daughter."

The team watched from the steps as the limo drove away.

Lila walked over to John. "Where is Zeke?" she asked.

"Danni asked us to find her friend Clara. Zeke found Clara and ten other girls. They are on their way home," said John, opening the briefcase.

"I'm so glad," said Riley with a sigh.

"Let's count it," John suggested. "Five, ten ..." It only took a few minutes for John to count the money, wrapped in five-thousand-dollar bundles.

"Wow, a hundred and twenty-five thousand dollars," said Lila in amazement.

John picked up a piece of paper resting in the briefcase. "Here's a note." He read, "Thank you for finding my friend Clara. Love, Danni."

The group looked at each other.

"Have other girls already been rescued?" asked Lila.

John's cell phone rang. "This is John." He turned on the speaker. "This is Zeke."

"Return to J Bar J, Zeke."

"Do we ever get a rest?" asked a surprised Riley.

"We took fourteen girls away from the vineyards and returned them to their families. I call that a victory—small, but a victory," said John. He was silent for a long minute. "The FBI and federal Mexican police mounted a search sting. An informant led them to a small farmhouse near the border. Eight other young American girls were found. The families will have their children back in one or two days."

Riley and Lila breathed a sigh of relief.

"Was Zeke the informant?" asked Lila.

John smiled. "Perhaps. Now everyone get ready. We have a bank to visit this morning."

***

Jake Logan slammed his fist on the desk. "How did the police find those fifth graders so fast?"

Chip scratched his head. "You always said see the facts."

"The fact is, Munge is outraged. The only way those girls were rescued was because why?"

"Somebody talked," said Chip.

"Worse, somebody snitched on us. Let's set a trap, but tell no one," said Jake.

"Okay, boss."

"Now let's get busy on our next project. Call Allen in."

Chip opened the door and called for him. Allen stepped into the room.

"You and Chip will run the next money project. You have twenty-four hours to set it up. Dismissed."

CHAPTER 8

—

Mini-Suzie

When living life,
expect the unexpected.
—Sensei J. R. Jensen

John set down his phone, pressed the intercom button, and said, "Team Cacomistle to the conference room."

Riley, Lila, Chet, Nathan, and Roy walked into the room.

Riley nudged Lila. "What is a cacomistle?"

"It's a wild gray animal related to the raccoon. The ringed tail is as long as its body. One species weighs two to three pounds. The other species weighs twenty to twenty-five pounds. They live in the Southwest and Mexico."

"Really?"

"Yes, and they hunt at night," said Lila.

"We have three days to prepare our next mission," said John.

"Great. Our mole is on the job," said Zeke.

"Mole?" asked Riley.

"We have a helper among the ruffians." Nathan winked.

***

Chip walked into Jake's office with a large suitcase.

"Welcome. Get started now," said Jake.

Chip set up the equipment and stuck out a wand connected to the equipment.

"A new bug seeker?" asked Jake.

"Brand-new." Chip scanned the entire room, walking slowly. He took nearly thirty minutes. "We only have one bug. It's in the phone."

"Let's set the trap for our listeners."

"A trap?"

"Don't we have a bank job in three days?" said Jake.

"Yeah, and we need the cash flow," said Chip.

Jake picked up the phone and dialed. "Hey, Mike. Send me Mini-Suzie." He hung up.

***

A van drove up to the Logan residence, and a man placed a suitcase on the porch. He rang the bell and left.

Jake opened the door, carried in the suitcase, opened it, and pulled out a table clock. Flipping a switch on the side of the clock, Jake placed it on a shelf overlooking his desk and the wall phone plug connector.

"Now we'll see who we get for a visitor." Jake pulled out the telephone jack, placed the connector in the socket, but didn't push it in far enough to make the connection. He picked up the telephone and listened; it was dead.

***

John entered his office and noticed a red blinking light. He got on the intercom. "Zeke, our phone contact has gone dead. Take Lila's team to reconnoiter the bank."

The intercom came to life. "We're on our way."

***

Zeke drove the J Bar J van into town. He stopped at the post office and picked up the mail; at the grocery store, he bought cottage cheese and paprika. Parking next to the bank, he briefed the team on the next activity. Finally, he went to the flower shop for tall bluebell flowers. Zeke drove the team home with his purchases.

***

Late at night, a stealthy figure crept into Jake's office. He checked the telephone, the mouthpiece, and the wall jack. He pushed in the wall jack and heard a click.

Chuckling, the figure slipped quietly out of the room.

***

"I never would have believed it," said Chip, watching the video.

"Me neither," said Jake.

"Now what?"

"Let's switch the twins. Get Tommy out of jail and put his rat brother, Allen, where he can't bother us."

Chip laughed.

"Tommy needs a visit from his lawyers," said Jake. "Make the switch the day of the bank job."

"How?"

"Put Allen to sleep in the visitor's room, and put Tommy's clothes on him to complete the switch."

"My pleasure."

***

The county jail building looked like it had been built before World War I. It needed a good coat of paint and a thorough cleaning.

Three well-dressed men with briefcases entered the Claremont Jail facility. One of them weighed over three hundred pounds.

"We represent the law firm of Lewis, Owen, and Dodge," said Allen in his wig disguise. He handed the desk sergeant a letter.

"So, who do you want to see?" asked the desk sergeant.

"Tommy."

The desk sergeant picked up a phone and dialed. "Take Tommy to the interview room. His legal reps are here." Hanging up, he pointed down the hall.

Chip led the way down the hall and entered the room, as directed by an officer. Gus "Ox" Chandler could barely squeeze sideways into the room.

Tommy entered through a second door. "Legal reps?"

Chip stuck a needle into Allen's arm. Allen collapsed.

"Tommy, go to the corner and strip. You are changing clothes with Allen," said Gus.

Tommy quickly stood in his stockings and underwear. "Smart. The camera doesn't show this corner."

Chip stripped Allen, aided by Gus.

"Allen has been tipping off the cops," said Chip.

"What?" said Tommy, putting on new clothes and a wig.

"Jake will show you the video later. Help me dress Allen," said Gus.

After Allen lay dressed in prison clothes, Gus opened the door and yelled, "Hey, Tommy has collapsed. Get someone in here to help him."

The first-aid team rushed in with a gurney, picked up the prisoner, and hurried down the hall.

The three "lawyers" exited the jail.

"It sure is nice to breathe fresh air," said Tommy, out on the sidewalk.

"We have a bank assignment soon," said Chip.

"Good, I could use some action right now." Tommy grinned.

***

The robbery morning, the bank had been opened for an hour. People came and went on their errands.

Chet, in disguise, drove the white van past the bank to the two barriers placed in front of the corner bakery next to the bank.

Roy, also in disguise, hopped out of the van and pulled the barrier aside so the white van could pull in and stop. He stuck his head through the open passenger window. "You all know what to do," he said. Roy slid the barrier back in place.

Roy, Betty, Lila, and Riley nodded in agreement.

The van's side door slid open, and three elderly women and one elderly man stepped onto the sidewalk. The elderly driver climbed back in and stayed with the van.

Lila nudged Riley. "You sure look like a sweet old lady," she whispered.

"Thanks, I think," whispered Riley. "So do you, Lila."

Four well-dressed young men carrying briefcases approached and entered the bank.

"Lila, one of those young men looks familiar," said Riley.

"It's Chip, Allen, and friends."

"Oh."

An armored truck pulled up to the bank. Immediately, security guards surrounded the truck with shotguns pointed to the sky.

Guards unloaded sacks onto a handcart and moved them into the bank.

As the money cart entered the bank, Lila and Riley passed the bakery and walked to the crosswalk. They stopped with other pedestrians until the light turned green, and they crossed the street. They stood in front of Norton's Department Store window.

"We'll stay here to watch what happens in the window's reflection," said Lila. "We're window shopping."

Betty and Roy crossed the street and entered Norton's. They immediately went to the back of the store, where the furniture department was having a special. They stood by an emergency door that led to the alley.

Lila and Riley wore hearing aids.

"We're in position," said Lila into her collar microphone.

"Time for me to go into the alley," said Riley.

Glancing casually around, Riley entered the alley. Taking metal spikes from her purse, she scattered them along the left wall. No matter how the three-point spikes landed, one spike stood straight up. She left the alley and rejoined Lila by the window.

"Alley spiked," said Riley into her collar mike.

CHAPTER 9

—

The Bank

Use the lowest level of force necessary
to escape a dangerous situation.
—Sensei J. R. Jensen

Inside the bank, a disguised Tommy sat with the new-accounts receptionist. "Millie, I've decided on the mountain scene for my checks," he said.

"Very well," said Millie, standing and blushing. She pulled out a folder showing sample bank checks.

The bank guards entered with the cart.

Tommy stood, pulled a hunting knife from his briefcase, reached over the desk, and pressed the knife against Millie's throat.

Her eyes grew large.

"Tell Daddy to surrender," Tommy whispered.

"Daddy," said Millie. "Help, surrender." Her voice, filled with terror, echoed throughout the bank. Customers, tellers, and bank guards stopped and looked at her.

Bank manager Joseph Allen looked at his daughter. "All weapons on the floor. Everyone on your stomachs on the floor. Now!" he commanded.

Security guards placed guns, pepper spray, and nightsticks on the floor. They lay down on their stomachs with hands behind their heads. Customers lay face down on the floor.

A well-dressed young man picked up all weapons and put them in his briefcase. He placed the briefcase on top of the cash-laden cart.

At the same time, two other well-dressed young men went to the tellers' cages and gathered up bundles of twenties, fifties, and hundred-dollar bills. The bills went into new attaché cases.

"I can help you," said a teller from her position on the floor.

"Stay down," Tommy hissed.

The teller didn't move.

Tommy held Millie's elbow and guided her to the bank door. She walked quietly; with a knife at her throat, she had no choice.

A horn sounded once outside the bank. The robbers immediately left the bank with the hand truck and attaché cases.

"No one follows," said Tommy, pushing Millie out the bank doors in front of him. As soon as the robbers disappeared, the bank manager reached over and pushed a button on his desk.

***

Outside the bank, a gray van stood with back and side doors open. As Tommy pulled Millie along the sidewalk, the money cart raced past him, and up metal rails connected to the van. The rails were detached, dropped on the asphalt, and abandoned.

Tommy pushed Millie through the van's side door and climbed in behind her. The others climbed in behind them.

"Go!" yelled Tommy when he saw the traffic light turn green. The gray van sped forward.

The white van shot out past the barriers and into traffic, the driver turning on his emergency flasher. The white van stopped and blocked any right turn.

"Take the alley," Tommy said calmly.

The gray van sped into the alley. The two left tires burst as they ran over the upturned spikes. The van crashed into the alley's brick wall with a sudden stop. Bodies flew forward.

Betty and Roy entered the alley from the rear of the store. Betty slid the van's side door open and pulled out the hostage, Millie.

"Go back to the bank," said Betty.

The dazed and bruised Millie stumbled back down the alley and moved into the dangerous area behind the crippled van.

Riley caught the girl and directed her to the opposite wall.

Putting Millie's hand on the wall, Riley said, "Stay left." She moved backward but watched until Millie moved out of the alley and stepped out of sight.

Tommy shook his head to clear away the sudden stop. He opened the rear van doors and wrapped his arms around Riley. "You'll do for a hostage," he said.

Riley shifted her weight to her right foot and swung her left elbow directly into Tommy's groin. Tommy doubled over. Reaching up, Riley grabbed Tommy's suit-coat sleeve. A sharp pull, and Tommy flew out of the van onto his back on the alley cement.

A spike pierced Tommy's right hand as he landed.

"Ouch," he groaned and grabbed his bleeding hand. His wig flopped onto the ground.

"Big Ears immobilized," said Riley into her collar.

Betty reached into the passenger window and put a compress on a bleeding head. She expertly wrapped a bandage over the compress, including the eyes.

"Passenger immobilized," Betty said into her headset.

Roy pulled a briefcase out of the van and carried it out of sight around the corner. In a moment, he returned with four sets of handcuffs.

Roy tossed one set of handcuffs to Chet. He picked up Tommy, pulled him around the corner, and pushed him left. "Take fifteen steps; enter the bar. Go to the left and sit in the farthest stool." Roy walked back around the corner to the van.

"Big Ears controlled," said Chet.

Betty took two handcuffs, reached through the window, cuffed the driver to the steering wheel, and cuffed the passenger to the driver's right wrist.

"Driver and passenger cuffed," Betty said.

Nathan entered the van with the fourth set of handcuffs. He flew backward out of the van. "Soo," he said, exhaling air just before he hit the alley floor.

The fourth robber pointed his revolver at Nathan.

Riley pulled three short steel rods from her sleeve and threw them directly at the gun hand. The rods hit the back of the hand holding the gun.

"Ahhh!" yelled the surprised robber. The gun dropped with a thud onto the alley floor.

Nathan threw the cuffs. Betty caught them and in a quick motion attached the robber's cuffed hand to the van's door handle.

"Fourth cuffed," said Betty into her collar mike. "It's time to leave. Doc to the Silver Bar Lounge."

Roy picked up the revolver and two briefcases and went around the corner of the building out of view.

Lila and Riley each picked up two cases from the van and followed Roy.

Betty followed immediately. The team entered a van waiting for them, closed the door, and the van pulled into traffic.

Roy emptied the revolver, putting the cartridges in his pocket.

***

Tommy took fifteen steps and slipped into the Silver Bar Lounge. Holding his hand, he walked over and sat on the farthest bar stool.

Katie entered the bar in a doctor's uniform, carrying a black bag. Seeing Tommy sitting at the bar, she walked over, opened her bag, and began cleaning the back of his hand.

Tommy sat silently.

"Yvonne, bring Allen a drink," said Katie.

Yvonne brought a cup of coffee and tea. "Tea or coffee?"

Tommy took the cup of tea. Katie finished bandaging the hand.

Yvonne reached over to the grill and brought back a plate of liver and onions and a hamburger with french fries.

Tommy took the hamburger and fries.

Katie put a different wig on Tommy's head. Yvonne handed Katie a jacket. Katie put the jacket on Tommy's shoulders.

"Stay here for fifteen minutes, eat, and then leave." Katie picked up the bloody materials, put them in a plastic bag, gripped her doctor's bag, and left, passing a police officer entering the lounge. "Hey, Yvonne, how long has that guy been here?"

"Half an hour, why?" asked Yvonne.

"Just curious," the police officer said and left.

***

Police cars stood at the bank with lights flashing. Additional police cars blocked the street. Police entered the alley and arrested the ruffians. Using heavy wire cutters, the police cut off the handcuffs, put the robbers in police vans, and drove away. The police called for a tow truck to pick up the disabled van in the alley.

***

Lieutenant Jim Mack and Sergeant Nolan Taylor began questioning the bank manager and his daughter. "Tell us what happened," said Mack.

"Well, a man said he wanted to open a checking account. Next thing I know, he has a knife at my throat, the bank is robbed, he walks me out to a van, he forces me to get in, and the van takes off. We drove into the alley by Norton's Department Store," said Millie.

"Go on," said Taylor.

"In the alley, the van crashed into a wall. Three or four people took control of the robbers. One old lady got me out of the van, directed me along the alley until I reached the street. By the time I crossed the street to the bank, police cars had arrived." Millie blinked back tears.

"Take Miss Allen to the station and have her give descriptions to our sketch artist," said Mack.

A police officer walked up to him. "Hey, Lieutenant, you've gotta see what we found in the alley."

Mack and Nolan left the bank and crossed the street to the alley. A police investigator handed the lieutenant a jack.

"This is what flattened the two left tires on the van," said the officer.

"Someone was well prepared," said Nolan.

"Cordon off the alley. We need to see if there are more jacks," said the lieutenant.

***

Katie entered the hospital and walked to her office. She dialed her office phone.

"Message for John. The man injured in the bank robbery was not Allen. He drank tea and ate a hamburger." Katie hung up the phone.

***

The dispensary worker at the jail checked the vital signs of the prisoner.

"Vital signs crashing. He's not responding. Put him on oxygen and get him to the hospital at once."

The first-aid team rushed the gurney to the ambulance, which drove away with siren blaring.

***

At the police station, Detective Tiffany Smith watched a fax machine stop. She tore off the report and walked into Lieutenant Jim Mack's office.

"It's just as you suspected: eight incidents of bank robbery in four states. Over three hundred thousand dollars taken in each incident," she said.

"What results?"

"Seven robberies failed. The police captured the robbers—all ruffians. They figure only one robber in our city escaped."

Lieutenant Mack scratched his head. "And?"

"Eyewitnesses said small groups captured the robbers. They were dressed as elderly people. Probably two females and two males—martial-arts types, probably eighteen to twenty-four years old, trained, very effective," said Tiffany.

"And over two million dollars stolen," Jim read from the report.

"Yes, but all the money was recovered from the other robberies." A phone rang. Detective Smith answered and listened. "We now have the money from today's robbery," she told the lieutenant.

Lieutenant Mack shook his head in wonder.

"So, we have four people, well trained, stopping bank robbers, including our bank. It seems we have unknown helpers we know nothing about. Let's find them."

CHAPTER 10

Allen

Each talent you learn
opens another door.
—Sensei J. R. Jensen

Riley paced back and forth between the dining table and the french doors.

"I blew it on this assignment," she said. "I'm sorry."

John rose. "When we placed that electronic bug in Lyman's house, we knew the dangers."

"But ..."

"Did the hostage get clear?"

"Yes, she ..." said Riley.

"Did the robbers remain at the scene until the police arrived?" asked John.

"Police caught the ruffians," said Lila. "Allen escaped."

"Your assignment was to free the hostage, which you did," said John.

"But when Nathan came flying out of the van backward and a gun appeared?" Riley shuddered.

"Yeah, nice throw with the rods, Riley." Nathan laughed.

"Yeah, thanks, Riley," said Lila, forcing herself to relax.

Riley visibly relaxed.

The others smiled.

John played Katie's telephone message.

"Tommy was in jail. It must have been him who robbed the bank, which means Allen was traded for Tommy at jail."

"So where is Allen?" asked Lila.

***

Tommy entered Jake's office.

"What's with the disguise?" asked Jake, seated in his chair.

"We took the bank. A van blocked our escape, so we went down the alley. Flat tires, handcuffs, and old farts appeared."

"What?"

"Those old farts thought I was Allen. I went next door to a bar. A doctor bandaged my hand. They gave me this disguise, plus tea to drink and a hamburger to eat," said Tommy.

"Did you know the doctor?" asked Jake.

"Nope."

"A cop came to the bar, and the barmaid said I had been there for half an hour. The cop left. What is going on?"

"We're in trouble. Begin the emergency escape plan."

Tommy pulled out a drawer and filled his hand with an automatic pistol and two clips of ammunition. He followed Jake out the back door to the jeep. They entered the back alley. In minutes, they drove a jeep on the highway headed out of town.

***

The ambulance drove into the emergency entrance. Nurses and EMTs hurried the gurney into room nine, nearest the door.

Katie met the gurney. She blinked when she saw the patient. Checking his eyes, she said, "Check his body for puncture wounds. Blood work stat. Toxicology stat."

Nurses hurried to comply with the doctor's orders.

***

Katie sat by Allen's bed. An IV was strapped to his arm. Fluids flowed wide open.

Katie dialed the room phone. "Message for John. Allen is in the hospital ICU. His twin was at the bar, where I bandaged the back of his hand. Call me."

***

John hung up the phone. He pressed a buzzer on his desk and patiently waited.

Within ten minutes, Lila, Riley, Roy, and Chet entered the office and sat down.

"What's up, JJ?" asked Lila.

"First, we have been receiving many requests for help. The latest was a lost child in Grover Canyon, which turned out to be false. Second, we received a request for surveillance from a businessman who doesn't exist."

"What does this all mean?" asked Lila.

"Logan has found out Allen is our spy. He took a group into the jail, drugged Allen, and switched him for his twin brother, Tommy."

"Which means Tommy was at the bank," said Roy.

"Allen and Tommy are twins. John sent Tommy to jail for drug trafficking," Lila whispered to Riley.

"Tell me about Riley since she got here," said John.

"Well, on the first day, we helped her get away from the ruffians. Riley did the bear-hug escape. And at the bank, she did the same bear-hug escape when grabbed by the guy in the van."

John sat and twiddled with a pen, thinking. "When Riley arrived, who did she fight?"

"Chip."

"And who did she fight in the alley?"

"Allen, or rather Tommy."

"Our enemies have figured out that we are causing them

problems," he said. "Lyman is trying to keep us busy to miss his real targets."

"What do we do?" asked Nathan.

"Third, Katie called. She fixed an injured hand. The young man ordered tea; then he ate a hamburger and fries at the bar."

"So?" asked Riley.

"The recognition code is no drink and order both meals," said Roy.

"Both meals?" asked Riley.

"It's to make sure we have a team member getting first aid," said John.

"Allen is in the hospital," said Chet.

Lila clicked her fingers. "Wasn't Allen assigned to keep tabs on Senator Davis?"

John shook his head. "Allen was assigned to the bank job, so Logan sent someone else to watch Senator Davis. Allen got wind of Senator Arlow Davis being watched by Jake Lyman and his ruffians. He called me, and I sent Matthew to scout the situation. Matthew was hurt but escaped. He was in a hospital for nearly two days, sent me a coded message by his backup, Penny, and disappeared."

John drummed his fingers on his desk. "Penny called and said Matthew will arrive in two hours with a skinhead following him. We report to Liberty Park in ninety minutes. Riley, again, stick close to Lila. Get your park escaping gear. Dismissed."

Lila led the way out to the storage room. She handed Riley a small satchel. "This will be your disguise for our park adventure."

"More intrigue? Fun," Riley said.

"Fun? Yes, but dangerous. The ruffians don't play fair. We must be on our toes or someone in the park will get hurt."

***

Lieutenant Jim Mack signed his name on a report and threw it into the OUT basket.

Tiffany walked into the room and handed him a second report.

"Before you leave on vacation, here's another report on a kid hurt by a gang of ruffians in New Mexico."

"So?"

"Our friend Chip was the skinhead identified as the perp."

"What happened to the kid?" asked Mack.

"That's just it. The kid was in the hospital, and then he disappeared. And the skinhead, Chip, disappeared too."

"What?"

"The kid hurt in New Mexico was last seen boarding a bus heading west."

"Toward us?"

"Yes."

***

Roy hung up the phone and joined Chet, Lila, and Riley.

"Matthew will arrive shortly. Take separate routes to Liberty Park. Expect anything, but follow the basic plan."

"Who drives the van?" asked Chet.

"John. Katie will be in the van to give Matthew the medical help he needs. Our team and Matthew's team will cover the getaway," said Roy.

"Who is Katie?" whispered Riley.

"She is a doctor John helped out of a mess last year. She insists on helping our injured team members," whispered Lila.

"We meet at the rendezvous point after we leave the park," said Roy.

"Or find our own way home," said Lila.

***

A mother and her two kids played on the swings in Liberty Park. Roy and Chet played Frisbee, being careful to stay near Lila, who pushed a baby carriage around.

Riley wore work clothes and cleaned up papers on the grass with a gripper stick.

Across the street, a bus pulled up and stopped. Several passengers climbed out, following the driver to get their suitcases.

"Code red. Fight at the park. Hurry." Chet hung up his cell phone.

Matthew Green appeared, holding his side, and limped across the street to the van, parked diagonally at the curb. Under the front tires were wedges. A young woman in a doctor's uniform helped Matthew into the back of the van and shut the doors.

***

A disguised Chip watched from a car parked on the edge of the park. "It's him. Block the van. Now," he instructed into a cell phone.

Three cars pulled out, blocking the back and both sides of the van.

The van pulled onto the wedges and shot over the curb, driving along the walkway.

Sprinklers turned on, and people scattered in all directions to escape the water.

Two cars jumped the curb and drove on the wet grass. The third car drove on the road, following the van.

Roy and Chet stopped playing Frisbee and dashed behind the escaping van, dropping blackjacks on the walkway.

The approaching cars ran over the blackjacks, and their front tires hissed flat.

The second car following the van hit a wet spot on the grass and sank up to the axles. The sudden stop bruised the occupants.

Lila turned the baby buggy at the last car. The buggy fired darts, and a rear tire on the third car popped and went flat.

Roy, Chet, and Riley walked away from the park; Lila followed with the baby buggy. They turned down an alley as two police cars, lights flashing, pulled up.

Chip watched the van move out of sight. "We'll get that bunch yet," he snarled.

CHAPTER 11

Train Ride

Train to move smoothly,
silently like a ghost.
—Sensei J. R. Jensen

Detective Smith walked into the office waving a report in her hand. "Whoever that group is, they left a lot of flat tires at Liberty Park."

"A very nice ambush in the middle of a busy park and no one hurt," agreed Lieutenant Mack.

"Chip and company were arrested in the park for driving on a public lawn," said Tiffany.

"Hmm. Lyman's ruffian squad was waiting for someone."

"Time to talk with our police chief?"

***

Lieutenant Mack and Detective Smith sat in front of Police Chief Dewey Rogers.

"I've called you in to discuss Lyman and his ruffians."

"Why have you kept us out of the loop on this one?" asked Lieutenant Mack.

"I have been working with a civilian contractor who has highly trained operatives. His budget makes our tax funds look like a piggy bank."

"Who pays the contractor?" asked Detective Smith.

"That's just it. The contractor works for donations," said Chief Rogers. "I have been told to assign you two on the next case."

A knock sounded at the door.

"Come in, Senator Davis."

"Thank you, Chief Rogers. How do you plan to keep my daughter and granddaughter safe?"

"Are you acquainted with John Johnson of the J Bar J?"

"No."

"He and his team will stay close to your family and protect them. My team will shadow Jake Logan and his ruffians."

"Will that be enough?" Senator Davis stared into Chief Rogers's eyes.

"We think so."

***

Donna entered the ranch's living room and handed John a manila envelope. "Here are the tickets you requested," she said.

"Thank you, Donna." With everyone seated, John opened the envelope and passed out smaller envelopes to the entire team. "Our phone bug at Logan's business has gone inactive, but before that occurred, we got information about Senator Davis. The information included a train trip the senator's daughter, Martha, and granddaughter, Josie, plan to take."

"What do you think is going on?" asked Roy.

"It's just a guess, but I think our ruffians are planning a kidnapping party for Josie and then blackmail Senator Davis into doing something for Lyman. Ideas?"

Roy handed each person a photograph of a woman in her late thirties and a girl, age twelve, with light-brown hair, blue eyes, and dimples—a train ticket, and another smaller white envelope with twenty-dollar bills inside.

"What does Lyman want?" asked Lila.

"We don't know. We must find out and alert Mr. Johnson," said Roy.

"And all this money to spend on what?" asked Riley, money visible in her hand.

"Food, necessities, emergencies," said Roy.

"Emergency on a train? How quaint," said Lila.

"Lila, you and Riley get set up with traveling bras."

"Bras?" whispered Riley. Lila just laughed.

Without warning, John leaped out of his chair and tipped back Chet's chair. Chet easily slid out of his chair and moved by the door for a quick escape.

"Expect the unexpected," said John tipping the chair upright. Smiling, he left the room.

***

Riley sat on her bed. Lila pulled out two boxes from their closet.

"Just when you think you've got it figured out, JJ throws us a curve," said Lila.

"He's good at that," agreed Riley.

Lila motioned to the boxes. Each girl opened a box and pulled out an oversized bra.

"We're supposed to wear these?" asked Riley.

"Only on special assignments. Watch me." Lila pulled a long metal rod from the front of the bra. Next, she pulled a miniature bow string stuck inside the bra strap.

"Now be careful to slide out the arrows." Lila slid three mini-arrows from the bra straps. "Twist the arrow." Artificial feathers slid into view.

"Nice," said Riley.

"These are nursing bras. John just had to have his fun." Lila opened the front of the bras and pulled out four small, round discs. "The silver discs are flash-bang devices to confuse others while you get away. The golden discs are tear-gas canisters." Lila pulled two nose plugs from the center of the bra. "Try to put in the nose plugs before you release the gas."

"How do I activate the canisters?"

"Just throw them against anything hard."

The phone rang. Lila picked it up and listened.

"John wants you to wear the mountain pack, and I get to wear the desert pack on the train," she said.

"John really wants us to be prepared," said Riley.

"Let's activate our GPS," said Lila.

***

The train platform was busy with passengers boarding the train and settling into their staterooms.

Soon the conductor called out "Board!" and the train moved out of the station.

Lila and Riley settled in their stateroom for a short nap.

The rest of the team, Chet and Roy, went directly to the dining car for a snack.

***

A sharp knock at the door woke Lila and Riley.

Lila looked at her watch. "We've overslept. That was Roy telling us Martha Adams and her daughter, Josie, have entered the dining car for dinner."

"Why did he knock so hard?" asked Riley.

"It's a prearranged signal to tell us the club car is almost full. If we want to meet them, we better hurry."

The two young ladies left their stateroom and ran to the dining car.

Stepping into the car, Riley spotted Josie and her mother. Their table had two empty seats, and a couple was hurrying toward them.

Riley grabbed Lila's hand and pulled her to the table.

"May we eat with you?" Riley asked.

The other couple stopped, disappointed. A waiter came up to the disappointed couple and directed them to another table.

"Yes, please do." I'm Josie. This is my mom, Martha."

"I'm Riley, and this is Lila."

A waiter came to the table, placing plates of hot food in front of Josie and Martha.

"Wow, those look good. What are they called?" asked Lila.

"Our hamburger plate special," said the waiter.

Riley smiled at Lila. Lila nodded.

"Two of the same, please," said Riley.

"And to drink?"

"Lemonade," said Riley.

"Water," said Lila.

The waiter gave a slight bow and left.

Josie took a big bite of hamburger. "Mmm, good," she said.

"We're going to California to the beach," said Riley.

"We need suntans." Lila winked.

The waiter returned with drinks.

Josie swallowed. "We're going to visit my grandfather, Senator Arlow Davis. Have you heard of him?"

"Yes, he is well known," said Riley.

Martha opened her purse and brought out a bottle of pills.

"I wish they would put easy-open caps on these bottles." She struggled opening the bottle, and pills spilled all over the table.

"Oh my," said Martha, embarrassed.

Riley and Lila quickly covered the edges of the table. The pills just stopped against their hands and arms. Lila palmed one pill and dropped it into her lap.

"How clumsy of me. My heart pills. I always have to have them with me," said Martha.

The foursome rounded up the pills and put them back into the bottle.

Gently, Martha tipped the bottle so only one pill dropped into her hand. She popped the pill into her mouth and took a swallow of water from her glass.

"You two are very fast with your hands," said Josie, taking another bite while looking at Lila and Riley.

Lila took a napkin, pulled out a pen from her purse, dropped the pill from her lap into her purse, and began to draw. It was a cartoon of a heart swallowing a pill. She showed the napkin to Josie.

Josie laughed, took the napkin, and showed her mother. Martha laughed at the cartoon.

The waiter appeared and placed hot plates of food in front of Lila and Riley.

"This looks good," said Lila. She winked at Josie. "I'll show you how to make a simple cartoon ... after we eat."

"Deal," Josie agreed.

***

The train pulled into the Ridge Valley Station.

A group of people waited until passengers stepped off the train; then they boarded and moved to suites or day benches for a ride to their destination.

Four athletic young men boarded and went directly to the dining car.

Lila finished her drawing lesson and looked at Josie's completed cartoon.

"What do you think?" asked Josie.

"I think you have talent and need to keep at it," said Lila.

"We'll meet you at lunch," said Riley, standing up.

"Good-bye until later." Lila pushed back her chair and followed Riley out the door.

***

Tommy entered the dining car and approached Martha and Josie. "Are you finished with this table?" he asked.

"Oh yes," said Martha. Josie stood up and moved into the aisle.

Chip snatched the purse sitting on the table and sprinted to the open door. Tommy picked Josie up by the waist and hurried out the same open door.

"Mom!" screamed Josie.

"Josie! My purse! Someone help my daughter!"

The young men with Tommy blocked the aisle against anyone who rose and tried to interfere.

***

Riley and Lila stood between railroad cars when Tommy and Josie slipped out the door and jumped onto the station platform.

Riley hurried down the steps, knocked Tommy flat onto the train platform with the back of her hand, and quietly took Josie's hand.

Two athletic young men jumped down onto the train platform behind Riley and Josie. Tommy touched Josie's throat with a knife. Josie stopped struggling. Seeing the knife, Riley also stopped struggling.

"Take these two to the van," said Tommy.

***

Lila was caught in the press of bodies trying to exit the dining car. "Chet, Roy: Riley and Josie are on the station platform surrounded by ruffians," she said, talking into her collar communicator.

Lila returned to the dining car and walked over and sat by the distraught Martha.

"Martha, look out the window. Riley is with Josie. They will be all right."

"A man stole my daughter. I need the medicine in my purse," said Martha, looking out the window.

Lila reached into her purse, located the pill, and slid it next to the salt and pepper shakers.

"Oh, look. I see one of your pills." Lila pulled back the shakers, revealing the pill.

"Oh, I guess we missed it," said Martha. "I've got to get help for Josie."

Lila motioned to the waiter to approach. "Mrs. Adams's purse was stolen, and her daughter was kidnapped. Please call the police."

***

Tommy dropped Josie on her feet, closed his knife, and slid it into his pocket. "Walk. Be silent or my men will hurt your mom."

"Don't hurt my mom. She is nice," said Josie, upset but walking quietly.

"Who are you?" Tommy asked Riley.

"I'm Josie's cousin," she said, holding Josie's hand.

Chip walked behind.

Ruffians surrounded the small group. They left the platform, moved to a van with blacked-out windows, and forced Josie and Riley inside. They also entered and sat down.

"You're my cousin?" whispered Josie.

"Back to Noah's ark," Riley whispered back. Josie giggled despite the situation.

"No talking," instructed Tommy, rubbing his bandaged right hand.

The van drove away from the train station and into the main street.

Chip put paper sacks over Riley and Josie's heads. "Just keep your mouths shut."

Josie and Riley kept holding hands.

***

"Car four to team: stay at your site and give reports."

The comm link stayed silent for nearly ten seconds.

"Car ten, the van with blacked-out windows is on Main Street."

"Car twelve, white van passing Rosemont Drive."

"Car four, white van on the freeway at Dillingham."

"Eyes in the sky, white van heading west."

"Car eight, white van reversing direction and heading east."

"Eyes in the sky, white van on access road at Dillingham, turning north."

CHAPTER 12

The Farm

Giving up is someone else's job.
—Sensei J. R. Jensen

The van drove for nearly an hour on dusty roads until it reached a farmhouse. Workers were busy moving bales of hay from a flatbed truck to desired locations around the farmyard.

"Lock these two in the shed," said Tommy.

Without a word, the ruffians marched Riley and Josie into the tack shed.

"Give me your shoes and purses," said Chip.

The two girls complied. He threw the items in a satchel and carried it with him and then closed and locked the door.

"Let's go." The ruffians left the barn. Chip slipped out the door and hid behind hay bales. He waited and listened.

"Riley, what's going on?" asked Josie, trying not to cry.

"We have been kidnapped. I don't know why," said Riley.

"What can we do?"

"Be patient. We have people looking for us."

"Oh? Who?"

"My boss and friends."

***

"John, this is Roy."

"Go ahead, Roy."

"Josie and Riley were kidnapped. They were forced into a van and just vanished."

"Remember, Riley activated her GPS at the J Bar J. Get off the train. Get transportation, and head for her location," said John.

John picked up the phone and listened. He dialed another number. "Roy and Chet, drive on Highway 2333 to Logan's farm. Hook up with Allen. All other staff to the living room."

In a few minutes, all staff reported to the living room.

"What's up, John?" asked Donna.

The phone rang. "This is John." He listened and then hung up. "Josie and Riley have been taken to a farm about fifty miles north. Police are amassing as we speak. Jake Logan is going to jail."

"Can we do anything?" asked Donna.

"Not this time. The police are on the job. The other team members will arrive at the farm shortly. Now we wait."

CHAPTER 13

The Escape

Alive or nearly dead,
never give up.
—Sensei J. R. Jensen

Josie stamped her foot. "I hate it in here." She kicked the cage door, which rattled and shook.

"Interesting," said Riley, approaching the corner of the door.

"What's so interesting?"

Riley pushed hard on the door; it popped open.

"We're free," said Josie.

"It's too easy. Wait." Riley slipped out into the farmyard; Josie followed her. They hurried to the corner of the shed and peeked.

"What do you see?" asked Josie.

"A long run to the trees across a field. We need shoes," said Riley.

The two returned to the shed and searched in boxes and on shelves.

"No shoes," said Josie. "Just some old cowboy hats, saddles, harnesses, and an old pair of chaps."

"Bring the chaps over to the door. We can use the light coming through the window to make moccasins."

"You can make moccasins?"

"Search for something sharp to cut with," said Riley.

Both searched the shelves and boxes again for a sharp tool.

"Here is a hammer, nails, and a chisel," called out Josie.

"Great. Bring the chisel. It should do the trick." Laying out the chaps, Riley put her feet on the leather. "Josie, watch and listen for guards. We have to keep our moccasins a secret."

Josie moved over to the door.

Riley cut strips of leather off the chaps; she also cut slits in the edge of the moccasins. She wove the strips from slit to slit, standing on the cut-out leather. Pulling the strips together, Riley had her first moccasin. Repeating the process, she made another moccasin for her other foot.

"Josie, your turn."

Josie stood on the cut-out leather. In only minutes, Josie had moccasins tied on her feet.

"Riley, I hear footsteps outside the door."

Rolling up the chaps, Riley stuck them into a box. "Give me your moccasins."

Josie handed them to her.

Riley took her moccasins and Josie's, placed them in the box with the cut-up chaps, and put the box on a shelf.

The door opened. Tommy looked in at the two girls sitting on wooden crates. He threw two paper sacks onto the floor.

"Lunch." Tommy slammed and locked the door.

Josie was closest to the sacks. She reached over and picked them up. "Do we dare eat?"

"When in captivity, eat to keep up your strength," whispered Riley, peeking through the dirty door window.

Josie opened her sack and pulled out a cheese sandwich.

"Smell it."

Josie sniffed the sandwich. "It smells okay."

"Moccasins back on," said Riley.

Josie pulled down the box and handed Riley her moccasins; then Josie put on hers.

Riley also sniffed her sandwich. "Let's eat," she said, taking a bite. "We'll have to have a distraction before we try to escape."

"Like what?"

Riley looked out the window. "Like police cars driving up without their lights and sirens going. Let's run."

***

Dr. Katie looked at the toxicology report. Taking a tray with a needle and medicine bottle, she went into Allen's room.

"How do you feel?" she asked.

"Like I've been run over with a lawnmower," said Allen.

"What did you do when you went into the bar by the bank?" asked Dr. Katie.

"I haven't been to the bar in weeks."

"At the bar, I bandaged the back of your right hand."

Allen looked at his right hand; the skin was clear and untouched.

"It must have been my twin brother, Tommy."

"The hospital record says you are Tommy. You have a police guard outside the door."

Dr. Katie gave Allen a shot.

"What will the shot do?" he asked.

"In ten seconds, you'll be able to run the hundred-yard dash in eight seconds flat." She went to a door inside the room and swiped her nametag. The door light blinked from red to green. Pushing the door open, Dr. Katie motioned for Allen to follow.

Allen got out of bed, flexing his muscles. "Where are we going?"

"To my car. We'll call John and find out the plan."

***

Chip glanced out the farm window.

"Our hostages are running across the field, just as we planned"

"Well, go catch them," said Jake.

Chip and Tommy raced out the door just as the phone rang.

Jake walked over and answered. "Hello."

"You have police cars coming from all directions. Get out." The phone clicked off.

***

Tommy and Chip raced after the girls. "Stop!" Chip shouted.

"Don't stop," said Riley, running into the trees. She stopped behind a row of bushes. Josie stopped when she saw Riley.

"What are you doing?"

"Hide behind these bushes." Riley pulled off her blouse.

Josie blinked in surprise.

Pulling two arrows, a rod, and a bow string out of her bra, Riley made her miniature bow. She twisted the arrow to get feathers, nocked an arrow, and, after putting her blouse back on, waited.

Chip ran into the trees and stopped to listen.

Riley pulled back her bow string and let it fly, smoothly pulling out a second arrow.

"Ouch!" The arrow stuck in the back of Chip's arm. In seconds, he slumped to the ground.

Tommy dove over the bush and pushed Riley down. Rolling away from Tommy, she leaped up, swinging the tiny bow and arrow at him.

"Give it up." Tommy laughed. He clamped onto Riley's left arm; she scratched his arm with her arrow.

Tommy wrapped his arm around her neck, stumbled, and fell to the ground.

"What happened?" asked Josie.

"We are really free." Riley smiled reassuringly.

***

Jake Logan opened the door to the basement. He went down the steps and hurried to a closet. Pulling open the door, he stepped inside, flipped on the light switch, and a motor opened another door. He stepped inside a second closet, which led to a tunnel under the farm. Grabbing a flashlight off the wall, he hurried down the tunnel.

***

Police cars entered the farm yard. Police hurried into the farm buildings.

Josie and Riley waved to the police from the edge of the trees.

The police hurried over and were surprised to see Chip and Tommy asleep on the ground. They cuffed the pair.

Police carried the sleeping, handcuffed Tommy and Chip to a police car. It took four husky policemen to carry each of them.

CHAPTER 14

Farewell

The entire staff settled down in the living room on the J Bar J. John raised his hands for silence.

"The good news is Josie is safe. We're not sure what Jake Logan had in mind on this kidnapping, but he escaped. The police found a tunnel that led under the farmhouse to a hillside garage. The garage was well hidden among trees and bushes."

Donna came in with a tray of vegetable drinks. "Get them while they're cold."

"You do well, Donna," said Lila.

"Appreciation always welcomed," said Donna.

"Even better, Logan is on the FBI list of wanted bank robbers. And the bank donated money to our article forty-seven some twenty-five thousand dollars," said John.

The group cheered.

"We have one sad note," said John. "Riley will be going home and starting school next week."

"You're making us do all the work," said Lila with a straight face.

"I'll miss you too, roommate," said Riley, choked up. Then she smiled. "There is always next summer."

Riley picked up her suitcase, put her pack on her back, and followed Donna to the J Bar J van in the yard. In less than a minute, the van drove away.

"How did Riley get accepted to the university so fast?" asked Lila.

"JJ," answered a chorus of voices.

"But why?" asked Lila.

John put on his cheesy grin. "You know me pretty well."

"So, Riley is on assignment. She just doesn't know it yet. Right?" asked Nathan.

"Perhaps. We need to set up our classroom with the map of the university campus," said John.

"On it," said Lila, hurrying from the room.

John dialed a number on his cell phone. "Training for the university assignment has begun."

> The end of one adventure
> Is the beginning of the next one.
> —Sensei J.R. Jensen